Awful End

Over two metres in height, with a bushy beard, Philip Ardagh is not only very tall and very hairy but has also written over fifty children's books for all ages, but nothing quite like *Awful End* . . . until now.

Currently living as a full-time writer with a wife and two cats in a seaside town somewhere in England, he has been – amongst other things – an advertising copywriter, a hospital cleaner, a (highly unqualified) librarian, and a reader for the blind.

'Philip Ardagh is a very, very, *very* funny man. I've been waiting for him to write an adventure story for ages, and here it is. It's brilliant, it's daft, and it'll make you LAUGH!'

VIVIAN FRENCH

by the same author
published by Faber & Faber

FICTION

The Eddie Dickens Trilogy
Awful End
Dreadful Acts
Terrible Times

Unlikely Exploits
The Fall of Fergal
Heir of Mystery
The Rise of the House of McNally

NON-FICTION

The Hieroglyphs Handbook
Teach Yourself Ancient Egyptian

The Archaeologist's Handbook
The Insider's Guide to Digging Up the Past

Did Dinosaurs Snore?
100$\frac{1}{2}$ Questions about Dinosaurs Answered

Why Are Castles Castle-Shaped?
100$\frac{1}{2}$ Questions about Castles Answered

PHILIP ARDAGH
Awful End

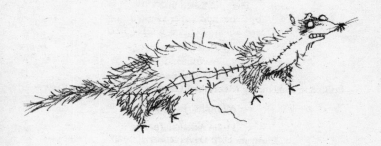

illustrated by David Roberts

faber and faber

First published in 2000
by Faber and Faber Limited
3 Queen Square London WC1N 3AU

Typeset by Faber and Faber
Printed in England by Mackays of Chatham plc, Chatham, Kent

A CIP record for this book
is available from the British Library

ISBN 978-0-571-20354-3

18 20 19

A Message from the Author

At no extra cost

Awful End was originally written in instalments, which explains why the chapters are called 'episodes' and not 'chapters'. These episodes were sent to my nephew, Ben, at boarding school, where they were – to my surprise – read out loud by his housemaster and housemistress 'Pa and Ma Brown'. This book is dedicated to them and (in alphabetical order) to: Cordelia, Francesca, Hattie, Henry, Isabelle, Katie and Ted Riley too. May their lives, and yours, be full of silly adventures.

PHILIP ARDAGH
England
2000

Contents

Crinkly Around the Edges

*In which Eddie Dickens is sent
away for his own good*

When Eddie Dickens was eleven years old, both his parents caught some awful disease that made them turn yellow, go a bit crinkly round the edges, and smell of old hot-water bottles.

There were lots of diseases like that in those days. Perhaps it had something to do with all that thick fog, those knobbly cobbled streets and the fact that everyone went everywhere by horse . . . even to the bathroom. Who knows?

'It's very contagious,' said his father.

'And catching,' said his mother, sucking on an ice cube shaped like a famous general.

They were in Eddie's parents' bedroom, which was very dark and dingy and had no furniture in it except for a large double bed, an even larger wardrobe, and thirty-two different types of chair designed to make you sit up straight even if your wrists were handcuffed to your ankles.

'Why are you sucking an ice cube shaped like a famous general?' Eddie asked his parents, who were propped up against piles of pillows in their impressively ugly double bed.

'Doctor Muffin says that it helps with the swelling,' said his mother. In fact, because she had a famous-general-shaped ice cube in her mouth, what she actually said was, 'Dotter Muffin schez va it hewlpz wiva schwelln,' but Eddie managed to translate.

'What swelling?' he asked politely.

His mother shrugged, then suddenly looked even more yellow and even more crinkly round the edges.

'And why do they have to be famous-general-shaped?' asked Eddie. He always asked lots of questions and whenever he asked lots of questions his father would say: 'Questions! Questions!'

'Questions! Questions!' said his father.

Told you.

'But why a famous general?' Eddie repeated. 'Surely the shape of the ice cube can't make any difference?'

'Schows sow muck chew no,' muttered his

2

mother, which meant (and still means), 'Shows how much you know.'

His father rustled the bedclothes. 'One does not question the good doctor,' he said. 'Especially when one is a child.' He was a small man except for when he was sitting up in bed. In this position, he looked extremely tall.

Then Eddie's mother rustled the bedclothes. It was easy to make them rustle because they were made entirely from brown paper bags glued together with those extra strips of gummed paper you sometimes get if you buy more than one stamp at the post office.

Postage stamps were a pretty new idea back then, and everyone – except for a great-great-great-aunt on my mother's side of the family – was excited about them.

One good thing about there being so few stamps in those days was that no one had yet come up with the idea of collecting them and sticking them in albums and being really boring about them. Stamp collectors didn't exist. Another good thing about there being no stamp collectors was that English teachers couldn't sneak up on some defenceless child and ask it* how to spell 'philatelist'.

* Teachers even thought of a child as 'it' back then. Some things never change.

Anyhow, even for those days, having brown paper bedclothes wasn't exactly usual. Quite the opposite, in fact. Bedclothes used to be an even grander affair then than they are now.

There were no polyester-filled duvets with separate washable covers. Oh, no. Back then there were underblankets and undersheets and top sheets and middle sheets and seven different kinds of overblankets. These ranged from ones thicker than a plank of wood (but not so soft) to ones which had holes in them that were supposed to be there.

To make a bed properly, the average chambermaid went through six to eight weeks' training at a special camp. Even then, not all of them finished the course and those that didn't finish spent the rest of their working lives living in cupboards under stairs.

The cupboard under the stairs of the Dickens household was occupied by Gibbering Jane. She spent her days in the darkness, alongside a variety of mops, buckets and brooms, mumbling about 'hospital corners' and 'ruckled chenille'. She never came out, and was fed slices of ham and any other food that was thin enough to slip under the bottom of the door.

The reason why Mr and Mrs Dickens had rustling brown paper sheets and blankets was that this was a part of the Treatment. Dr Muffin was always giving very strict instructions about the Treatment.

The smell of old hot-water bottles had almost reached 'unbearable' on Eddie's what-I'm-prepared-to-breathe scale, and he held his hanky up to his face.

'You'll have to leave the room, my boy,' said his father.

'You'll have to leave the house,' said his mother. 'We can't risk you going all yellow and crinkly and smelling horrible. It would be a terrible waste of all that money we spent on turning you into a little gentleman.'

'Which is why we're sending you to stay with Mad Uncle Jack,' his father explained.

'I didn't know I had a Mad Uncle Jack,' gasped Eddie. He'd never heard of him. He sounded rather an exciting relative to have.

'I didn't say *your* Mad Uncle Jack. He's *my* Mad Uncle Jack,' said his father. 'I do wish you'd listen. That makes him your great-uncle.'

'Oh,' said Eddie disappointed. 'You mean Mad *Great*-uncle Jack.' Then he realised that he hadn't heard of him either and he sounded just as exciting as the other one. 'When will I meet him?'

'He's in the wardrobe,' said his mother, pointing at the huge wardrobe at the foot of the bed, in case her son had forgotten what a wardrobe looked like.

Eddie Dickens pulled open the door to the wardrobe, gingerly. (It was a ginger wardrobe.)

Inside, amongst his mother's dresses, stood a very, very, very tall and very, very, very thin man with a nose that made a parrot's beak look not so beaky. 'Hullo,' he said, with a 'u' and not with an 'e'. It was very definitely a 'hullo' not a 'hello'. Mad Uncle Jack put out his hand.

Eddie shook it. His little gentleman lessons hadn't been completely wasted.

Mad Uncle Jack stepped out of the wardrobe and onto an oval mat knitted by children from St Horrid's Home for Grateful Orphans. Remember that place: St Horrid's Home for Grateful Orphans. There. I've written it out for you a second time. Never let it be said that I don't do anything for you. Remember the name. You'll come across it again one day, and probably between the covers of this book.

'So you are Edmund Dickens,' said Mad Uncle Jack, studying the boy.

'Yes, sir,' said Eddie, because his first name really was Edmund.

Eddie Dickens's father cleared his throat. He used a miniature version of the sort of brush the local sweep used to clear blocked chimneys. This was all a part of Dr Muffin's Treatment.

'Edmund,' said Mr Dickens, 'you are to go with my uncle and live with him until your dear, sweet mother and I –' he paused and kissed Mrs Dickens on the part of her face that was the least yellow and the least crinkly at the edges (a small section just behind her left ear) '– are well again. You must never wear anything green in his presence, you must always drink at least five glasses of lukewarm water a day, and you must always do as he says. Is that clear?'

'Yes, Father,' said Eddie.

'And, Jonathan,' added his mother, for Jonathan was the pet name she called Eddie when she couldn't remember his real one.

'Yes, Mother?'

'Do be careful to make sure that you're not mistaken for a runaway orphan and taken to the orphanage where you will then suffer cruelty, hardship and misery.'

'Don't worry, Mother. That'll never happen,' said Eddie Dickens, dismissing the idea as ridiculous.

If only he'd listened.

Mad Uncle Jack wanted to use the bathroom before he went and, being unfamiliar with the house, he found it difficult to get his horse up the stairs without knocking one or two family portraits off the wall.

The fact that he'd only nailed the portraits up there himself minutes before made it all the more annoying. He took the paintings with him whenever he strayed more than eleven miles from his house. Because his house was actually twelve miles from the nearest place, that meant he always had them with him.

A key part of the Treatment was that neither Mr Dickens nor his wife Mrs Dickens should leave their bed more than three times a day. Because they had both already been up twice that day, and both planned to get up later for an arm-wrestling competition against their friends and neighbours Mr and Mrs Thackery, who lived over at The Grange, neither of Eddie's parents could get up to see him off.

Instead, the bed was lowered from their window

on a winch constructed from the sheets that were no longer in use since the Treatment began.

'Good luck, my boy,' said Eddie's father. 'Under such extreme circumstances, I would kiss you, but I don't want you catching this.'

'Get well, Father,' said Eddie.

'Be good, Simon,' said his mother. Simon was the name Mrs Dickens used when she couldn't remember that his real name was Edmund or that his pet name was Jonathan. 'Be good.'

'I will,' said Eddie. 'Get well, Mother.'

It had started to rain and the raindrops mixed with the tears that poured down his mother's face. She was busy peeling an onion.

Episode 2

Even Madder Maud

In which Eddie first meets Malcolm . . .
or is it Sally?

When Eddie Dickens climbed into Mad Uncle Jack's covered carriage, he found that it was already occupied. In the corner, an elderly woman was stroking a stoat.

'You must be Malcolm,' said the old woman, with a voice that could grate cheese.

'No, madam. My name is Edmund,' said Eddie.

'I was talking to the stoat!' snarled the woman, pulling the creature closer to her. 'Well?' she demanded, staring at the animal.

The stoat said nothing. It didn't even twitch or blink. The woman seized it by the tail and held it aloft (which is in-those-days language for 'up a

11

bit'). It was as stiff as a board. 'Are you Malcolm?' she demanded.

It was round about then that Eddie Dickens realised that the woman must be completely crazy and that the animal must be completely stuffed. He took a seat opposite the woman.

'Put that seat back!' she screamed, so Eddie did as he was told and sat down.

Just then, Mad Uncle Jack stuck his thinnest of thin heads through the door of the carriage. 'Ignore her. She's quite mad,' he said gruffly.

'Who is she, sir?' asked Eddie.

'Sally Stoat,' said his great-uncle.

'Did she get her name from that stuffed animal she's hugging?' asked Eddie.

'It was the stoat I was referring to, you impudent whelp!' cried his great-uncle. 'That good lady is my wife, Mad Aunt Maud – your great-aunt – and there's most certainly nothing mad about her.'

Eddie's face went beetroot red. 'I do beg your pardon, Great-uncle,' Eddie spluttered. 'And you, Great-aunt,' he said, with terrible embarrassment. He hadn't even left the driveway of his own home and he had already managed to offend them both.

'Enough said,' said Mad Uncle Jack. 'I despise closed carriages so shall be lashing myself to the roof along with our luggage. I shall see you when we reach Awful End.'

'Awful End?'

'Our home. *Your* home, until your dear mother and father are cured of their terrible affliction,' Mad Uncle Jack explained.

Eddie's great-uncle clambered onto the roof where Eddie could hear him strapping himself into place next to his trunk.

'Drive on!' Mad Uncle Jack shouted.

Nothing happened.

'Driver!' he instructed. 'Drive on!' It was then that he must have remembered that they didn't *have* a driver. Eddie could hear him unstrapping himself and clambering across the roof above his head to take up position on the driver's chair.

Mad Uncle Jack gave a strange clicking noise that you sometimes hear people make to horses moments before they flick the reins and the carriage pulls off.

Eddie thought he even heard the flicking of the reins, but this was followed by silence except for the gentle patter of raindrops that were falling onto the stuffed stoat that his great-aunt was sticking out of the open window.

'Did you have a good war, dear?' she asked Eddie.

'What war was that, Great-aunt?' Eddie asked politely.

'How many have you been in?' she asked.

'None, as a matter of fact,' said Eddie. She was as tricky to talk to as her husband.

13

'Then don't be so particular!' she replied, pulling the stoat back into the dry of the carriage. 'Was Malcolm thirsty? Was he? Did he like his little drinky?'

'No horse!' called out a voice that Eddie recognised as belonging to his father, even though it sounded more yellow and crinkly at the edges than usual.

Eddie stood up and looked out of the window, across the driveway to his parents, who were sitting by the front door in their bed.

The weather wasn't doing their bedclothes much good. The brown paper bags looked a darker brown and were positively soggy. If his parents stayed out much longer, their bedding would soon turn to pulp. Eddie suspected that papier mâché wasn't a part of Dr Muffin's Treatment.

'No horse!' his father repeated, pointing to the front of the carriage.

Eddie climbed out, stepped onto the driveway and looked back at the carriage. He could see the problem. In the carriage sat Mad Aunt Maud with her stuffed stoat, by the name of either Malcolm or Sally, depending on who he was to believe. On the roof of the carriage were Eddie's trunk and his great-uncle's family portraits (that went with him always), and at the front of the carriage was his very thin and very mad Mad Uncle Jack, reins in one hand and a whip in the other.

But the problem was – and Mr Dickens had put it very well – that there was n-o h-o-r-s-e.

'Your great-uncle left him in the bathroom!' Mrs Dickens shouted, wiping away a tear from the corner of her eye. If the truth be told, what she actually shouted was: 'Yaw gway unk-le leff timinva barfroo,' because she had a whole peeled onion in her mouth.

A moment later, Mr Dickens's gentleman's gentleman led the horse out of the house and hitched him to Mad Uncle Jack's carriage.

15

'Thank you, Daphne,' said Mad Uncle Jack.

'Very good, sir,' replied the gentleman's gentleman. As a gentleman's gentleman, he knew that it was not his place to point out that he was not actually called 'Daphne' but 'Dawkins'. No, his place was a large basket in the kitchen with plenty of tissue paper, and he couldn't complain. Mr Thackery's gentleman's gentleman over at The Grange was far worse off. His place was on a small log behind a coal scuttle in the tackle room. Dawkins hadn't the slightest idea what a tackle room was, but had never thought to ask.

With the horse now in position, the carriage pulled away and they were off. Eddie waved out of the window at his parents until they became small dots in the distance. Perhaps this was part of their illness, or perhaps it was to do with perspective and it being a very long driveway.

'I think you should remove your clothes now,' said Mad Aunt Maud, as the carriage bumped along the wheel-ruts of an unmade-up road.

If Eddie Dickens had been beetroot red with embarrassment before, now he had gone blushing beetroot red. 'I beg your pardon?' he said, hoping that he hadn't heard her right.

He had. 'I said, I think you should remove your clothes,' she confirmed.

'Er . . . Why might that be, Mad Aunt Maud?' he

16

enquired as politely as possible, wishing that he was anywhere else in the whole wide world than in a carriage with this woman.

'If you wear all those clothes in here, you will have nothing to put on when we step out of the carriage, and then you will be cold,' said Mad Aunt Maud. 'I should have thought that was perfectly obvious.'

'But I'll be cold in here in the meantime, great-aunt,' Eddie was quick to point out.

Great-Aunt Maud glared at him. If looks could kill, he would have been seriously injured by this one. 'Have you ever thought of growing a moustache?' she asked suddenly.

'I'm only eleven –' Eddie protested.

'Quiet!' snapped Mad Aunt Mad. 'I was asking Malcolm here.' She gave the stuffed stoat a friendly rub between its glass eyes.

The stuffed stoat said nothing.

Eddie wondered if he'd be able to survive a whole journey sharing a carriage with this lunatic. At least she seemed to have forgotten about telling him to take his clothes off.

'Now, come on, young man,' said Mad Aunt Maud. 'Remove them at once!'

Eddie groaned.

To break the journey, Mad Uncle Jack stopped at a coaching inn called The Coaching Inn. It was in an unimaginative part of the countryside and to call

17

it anything other than The Coaching Inn might have confused both the locals and the passing trade.

Both the locals were there to greet Mad Uncle Jack's party. They were the landlord and landlady, Mr and Mrs Loaf.

Neither of them batted an eyelid when Eddie stepped from the carriage wearing nothing but his undershirt and a pair of long johns.

In those days, wearing nothing but your undershirt and long johns was considered being undressed. You couldn't really get much more naked than that. If there had been cinemas in those days – which there weren't – and they had shown a film of someone on the beach wearing nothing but his undershirt and long johns, there would have been outrage. Men with large beards

18

would have set up barricades and there would have been riots in the street.

Most people went through life without realising that they could actually remove their undershirts and long johns – they simply assumed that they were a part of them, like fingernails and hair. They simply assumed that these undergarments were their skin, made out of a different material from their face, hands and feet, and with buttons on them.

If anyone had appeared in just a pair of boxer shorts or swimming trunks, the womenfolk would have had 'an attack of the vapours' and the menfolk would have exploded in a rage at the indecency of it. What exactly 'an attack of the vapours' was is unclear, because there are no such thing as womenfolk any more, and there is certainly no such thing as an attack of the vapours.

If a person did suffer from such an attack in Eddie Dickens's day, however, it seemed to involve a high-pitched squeal, a swooning, and a falling to the ground (or floor) with much crumpling of the dress.

The way to assist a gentlewoman after such an attack was to wave a small bottle labelled 'SMELLING SALTS' beneath her nose.

As with an attack of the vapours, smelling salts don't exist today either. Nor do bath salts. Everyone uses bubble bath or shower gel instead, which is all very interesting.

As a result, when Eddie stepped out of the carriage outside The Coaching Inn coaching inn, he felt as naked as you would if you were completely in the nuddy (except, perhaps, for your watch), despite the fact that he was wearing more clothes than the rest of us would wear on an ordinary day at the seaside.

He, therefore, expected both of the locals – the landlord and landlady, Mr and Mrs Loaf – to be horrified. But not at all.

'This is Master Eddie,' Mad Uncle Jack explained, climbing down and standing beside his great-nephew. 'Please arrange to have him stabled, and arrange for two rooms – one for me and my good lady wife, and one for my horse.'

'Very good, Mad Mr Dickens,' said Mrs Loaf. She obviously knew Mad Uncle Jack well, but it would be rude to call him 'Mad Uncle Jack' because she wasn't one of the family. 'This way, please . . . though I do wish you weren't staying.'

While his great-aunt and great-uncle – and their horse – were shown to their rooms by his wife, Mr Loaf led Eddie to the stables.

'You'll sleep in here,' he said. 'There's plenty of straw, so you should be warm and comfortable.'

'But why should I have to sleep out here, while the horse gets to sleep in the inn?' asked Eddie, trying not to sound too pathetic and helpless.

'Perhaps your great-uncle can only afford two rooms,' the landlord suggested. 'And then there's the fact that he's completely mad.'

'Good point,' nodded Eddie, shivering a little.

'You know, Master Edmund, that great-uncle of yours never pays his bill,' Mr Loaf continued.

'Then why do you let him keep on staying here?' asked Eddie.

'Well, he sort of pays, see, but not with money,' said the man. He was carrying Eddie's trunk, which he now placed on a few bales of hay.

'He pays without money?' asked Eddie Dickens, frantically opening the trunk lid and pulling on the first garment he could find. It was one of Dr Muffin's chin-to-toe body stockings, which was knitted from coarse black wool and covered him up to his neck. He felt a lot less naked now. 'Then what does he pay with?'

'Well, usually with dried fish,' the landlord of The Coaching Inn explained. 'Two dried hake for a double room – per night – and half a halibut for a single room. I never asked him to pay in fish and I never said he could pay in fish, but pay in fish he always does.'

'So what do you do with all this dried fish?' asked Eddie, sitting on his trunk.

'I send it to your father and, knowing what rates I charge, and the method of fishology by which his uncle pays, he then converts the fish into money and sends me the exact amount.'

'You know my father?' asked Eddie excitedly. He had only been gone from his parents for half a day and he was missing them already. This was only the third time in his entire life that he had been away from home and it felt strange.

The first time he had been away from home was when he had been sent to sea. That was from when he was a year old to when he was old enough to go to school. The second time had been from when he was old enough to go to school until his tenth birthday. No wonder it felt so odd in that strange stable.

'No, I have never had the honour nor the privilege of meeting your father in person, Master Edmund,' said Mr Loaf, 'but we do communicate by post.'

'Aha!' said Eddie. 'That would explain the strange parcels my father so often takes to his study. I thought they smelt of dried fish.' His eyes lit up.

'Your eyes just lit up,' said the landlord in complete and utter amazement.

'No,' said Eddie. 'That was just a figure of speech.'

'I thought it had more to do with the body's electricity,' said Mr Loaf.

There was a lot of excitement about 'electricity' in those days before electric light, electric fridges and electric eels. That last one was a lie. There were most definitely electric eels way back then. How can we be so sure? Because Mad Uncle Jack would always tip Mrs Loaf with a dried electric eel at the end of each stay at The Coaching Inn. He was nothing if not generous and, as Mr Loaf so rightly said, completely mad.

Mister Pumblesnook

*In which Eddie is entranced
by a handkerchief*

Eddie found that the warmest place to lie was inside his trunk, but he couldn't sleep a wink. It wasn't because he was longer than the trunk, which meant that he'd had to curl himself into a ball. It wasn't because every ten minutes or so Mad Aunt Maud would burst into the stable, lift the lid of the trunk and scream, 'Not asleep yet?' in that terrible grating voice of hers, with wax dripping onto his face from her upheld candle. It had more to do with the fact that a band of strolling theatricals were rehearsing a play in the far corner of the stable.

Strolling theatricals were a strange breed of men and women who used to roam the countryside forcing unsuspecting yokels – who are locals who say 'ooh aar' instead of 'yes' – to watch something they called 'performances'.

A band of strolling theatricals was always led by a man called an actor-manager. You could always recognise an actor-manager from his large frame, from the fact that he always carried a slightly chipped silver-topped cane, from his booming, ridiculous voice – an actor-manager always used twenty-two words when one would do – and his blooming ridiculous name. Most actor-managers were called Mr Pumblesnook, and Mr Pumblesnook was no exception. He sat on a bale of hay in the corner of the stable of The Coaching Inn, barking instructions.

'Woof! Woof!' he said.

'Oooh, you weally aw such a funny man, husband deawest,' laughed his wife, who had a number of extremely irritating habits including pronouncing her 'r's as 'w's. If you don't think that's irritating, just you wait. By the time you reach the end of the next page you'll probably hate her as much as everyone else did.

'Oooh, you'we the most humowus fellow to have walked this eawth, husband deawest. Thewe hain't no denying it!' she added, which is a good example of three more of her irritating habits.

Mrs Pumblesnook began all her conversation with the word 'oooh' – usually with three 'o's – as well as sticking 'h's in front of words that didn't need them and – as if that weren't enough – she always called Mr Pumblesnook 'husband deawest' when she was talking to him.

So that deaf people weren't spared the irritation she caused, she had a number of awful visual habits too. Her face was covered with some of the reddest blotches ever to have graced the visage of any human being – this was in the days when people still had visages, remember – and Mrs P had the dreadful habit of picking at these blotches with her claw-like nails and putting any loose skin that came away in a special pocket sewn to the front of her dresses. Another awful habit was what she did with the skin later, but no matter how much you beg, you'll never get me to write that down. Never!!!

There was some disagreement as to how she came to have these blotches. Some of the strolling theatricals were convinced that she'd got them from drinking her husband's *Eyebrow Embrocation*, while others thought they were a result of wearing theatrical make-up every night for over forty years. What no one disputed was that collecting the flaky skin was quite the most repulsive thing imaginable.

But what of Mr Pumblesnook? He was busy

talking his theatricals through a difficult scene of their up-and-coming production.

'Remember! Attention to the smallest detail reaps the largest of rewards, my children!' he bellowed.

Eddie groaned. He was never going to sleep, so he might just as well give up. Bleary-eyed and more than a little grouchy, he climbed out of his trunk and wandered across the straw-strewn floor to watch the strolling theatricals at work.

'Observe closely the way in which I remove my kerchief from my pocket and give this simplest of acts new meaning and life,' Mr Pumblesnook pronounced. 'See how the production of said kerchief becomes more than a mere action and becomes an interpretation of the action itself.' Then, with a strange quiver, followed by a dramatic flourish, the actor-manager pulled a handkerchief out of his coat pocket.

The assembled company – including young Eddie Dickens – burst into spontaneous applause. Eddie had never seen anyone pull out a hanky in such a way . . . It had been dramatic . . . exciting . . . He had *cared* about that hanky.

'Oooh, we have han audience, husband deawest!' cried Mrs Pumblesnook, spying Eddie and breaking the magic. 'We have ha little gentleman hamong us!'

Mr Pumblesnook fixed a dramatic stare upon

the child. 'What is your name, boy?' he demanded.

'Please, sir,' said Eddie, 'it's Eddie Dickens.'

At that moment, Mad Aunt Maud marched into the stable and over to Eddie's trunk, a guttering candle clasped in her hand. She lifted the lid and, ignoring the fact that the trunk was obviously empty, shouted, 'Not asleep yet?' Without waiting for the reply that she wouldn't have received anyway, she dropped the lid with a 'thunk' then marched back out of the stable and into the night.

'Oooh, such a charming lady, husband deawest,' sighed Mrs Pumblesnook, looking after Eddie's great-aunt as though she were the beloved queen herself. 'Such wefinement and such bweeding.'

'Indeed,' agreed her husband. He turned back to Eddie. 'You are related to Mrs Dickens, I presume?'

Eddie nodded. For those readers who are concerned that we shall be lumbered with these oh-so-amusing theatricals for at least the remainder of the episode, fear not.

Fate would have it that a carelessly dropped match was soon to set fire to the surrounding hay and to the clothing of a number of the less important strolling theatricals.

Had this actually occurred during one of the 'performances', the show would have had to continue right through to the end, no matter the cost to human life.

One of the rules which such people lived by was that 'the show must go on'. This, however, was only a rehearsal, so, instead of Old Wiggins and Even Older Postlethwaite being burnt to a crisp, they fled into the courtyard of The Coaching Inn where their fellow theatricals beat out the flames with their jackets then proceeded to dunk them in the horses' drinking trough.

In the meantime (and in the stable) Mrs Pumblesnook picked at her facial blotches, and her husband practised rolling his eyes in a manner befitting a gentleman (for his upcoming leading role in *An Egg for Breakfast*).

Eddie had been quite forgotten in the excitement.

With a sigh, he climbed back into his trunk, closing the lid behind him. There he remained until daybreak.

On the Road Again

*In which Aunt Maud is even more
maddening than usual*

The journey to Awful End began bright and
early next morning. Mad Uncle Jack and
equally Mad Aunt Maud had breakfasted on
devilled kidneys, six eggs, a joint of ham and several glasses of port wine, served up by a jovial Mr
Loaf. Eddie had breakfasted on the lid of his
trunk. He'd had a slice of stale bread and some
mouldy cheese.

When Mrs Loaf had first appeared at the stable
with his food, the slice of bread had been fresh –
still warm from the oven where she had baked it –

and there hadn't been so much as a smidgen of mould on the generous slice of cheese. When Mrs Loaf realised this, she apologised most profusely (which means 'rather a lot' in the kind of language Mr Pumblesnook liked to use) and hurried back into the kitchen.

She returned with the stale bread and mouldy cheese, and apologised once more.

'Do forgive me, Master Edmund,' she said. 'I don't know what I was thinking. I can't have you go spreading stories about us treating our guests kindly now, can I? That way more people would come to stay and I'd never get a moment's peace.'

'I'm sorry?' said Eddie. He wasn't sure he understood.

'How would you like strangers sleeping in your house . . . and the moment one lot leaves another lot turns up?' she demanded.

'But surely that's what coaching inns are for?' began Eddie, only to be interrupted.

'It's all right for Mr Loaf. He doesn't have to do all that sheet-changing and washing and ironing. Oh, no. All he has to do is drink ale out of a pewter tankard at the bar and shout, "Time, gentlemen, please." That's all he has to do.'

'Then why do you work in an —?'

'So I don't want you feeling welcome, now do I?' she said, thrusting the stale-and-mouldy replacement breakfast onto the lid of the trunk. 'Eat this and be grateful.'

Eddie Dickens noticed that the plate had a large crack in it, clogged up with at least six months' worth of grime. This woman certainly knew how to make a meal unappetising when she put her mind to it.

'Thank you,' mumbled Eddie, more confused than ever.

If it was possible, and despite breakfast, Mad Uncle Jack looked even thinner than he had the previous day. He helped his wife and her stuffed stoat into the coach, shut the door behind Eddie, then clambered up into the driving seat.

Mr Loaf led the horse out of the main entrance to The Coaching Inn and hitched him up to the carriage.

'Thank you, my good man,' cried Mad Uncle Jack, reaching into the pocket of his coat and pulling out a dried eel, which he tossed down to the grateful landlord.

'No, thank *you*, sir,' said Mr Loaf and winked at Eddie Dickens, who was leaning out of the carriage window, watching the proceedings.

Eddie imagined Mr Loaf parcelling up the eel along with the other dried fish his great-uncle had used to pay for the board and lodgings and sending them on to his father.

'Goodbye, Master Edmund!' beamed the land-lord. 'Good luck!'

'Good riddance!' added Mrs Loaf, sweetly.

With a flick of the reins and a loud whinny – from Eddie's great-uncle, not the horse, which was still far too sleepy to be making conversation at that time of the morning – they were off.

Mr and Mrs Loaf ran alongside the carriage, shouting and waving at Eddie.

'Drop us a line, Master Edmund,' called the land-lord.

'Drop dead!' called the landlady.

'Stay again soon,' cried the landlord.

'Stay away!' cried the landlady.

'If you're ever passing this way –' began the landlord.

'Keep going without stopping,' finished the landlady.

And so the comments continued until the car-riage picked up speed and the Loafs were left behind them.

Eddie had to admit that Mrs Loaf really did have an excellent knack of making him feel unwelcome. He never wanted to go to The Coaching Inn again.

'What time is it?' demanded Mad Aunt Maud. She was looking directly at Eddie when she asked the question, so he decided that she really must be asking him and not the stuffed stoat.

'I'm afraid I don't have a watch,' said Eddie.

'Then borrow mine.' His great-aunt rummaged in a small patchwork sack she had on the seat next to her. She pulled out a silver pocket watch on a chain and handed it to him. 'Now, what time is it?'

He read the hands. 'It's three minutes after eight o'clock,' he said, passing the watch back to her.

She studied the timepiece in her gnarled hands. 'I couldn't accept this,' she said. 'It's solid silver.' She held the watch up to her right ear and listened. 'And it has a very expensive tick. No, I most certainly couldn't accept such a valuable gift from a mere child.'

'But it's yours,' Eddie tried to point out.

'No, I cannot accept it,' insisted Mad Aunt Maud sternly. 'We'll hear no more about it. What would your poor, crinkly-edged mother have to say about you trying to give away your treasured watch?'

Eddie sighed, but decided it was best not to try to argue with his great-aunt. He slipped the watch into his pocket.

'Thief!' cried Maud. 'Thief!' She brandished Malcolm the stuffed stoat by the tail, like a club. It was as stiff as a policeman's truncheon and made a frightening weapon. 'Return my property to me at once!' she demanded.

Eddie swallowed hard. He dug his hand back into his pocket and passed her back her watch.

Great-Aunt Maud grinned from ear to ear. 'What a charming present,' she said. 'How thoughtful. How sweet.'

Putting down Malcolm carefully on the seat next to her, she leaned to her left and opened the window of the carriage, then tossed out the silver fob watch. 'Useless trinket,' she mumbled.

There was a cry, followed by a bit of confusion and then the carriage lurched to a halt. Eddie was propelled out of his seat and – to his horror – landed head first in his great-aunt's lap.

Apologising, he got to his feet and caught sight of a bearded stranger through the open window of the carriage.

The bearded stranger was rubbing his head with one hand and holding Mad Aunt Maud's watch with the other.

Mad Uncle Jack jumped down off the now stationary carriage and was striding towards the man.

'Why did you cry out like that?' demanded Eddie's great-uncle. 'You frightened my horse.'

'Because one of your number assailed me with a projectile!' spluttered the bearded stranger, barely able to contain his rage.

'Who did what with a what?' demanded Uncle Jack.

'A member of your party assaulted me with a missile!' the bearded stranger explained. When it was obvious that Uncle Jack still had no idea what he was talking about, he tried again. 'One of your lot threw this pocket watch at me,' he said.

'How very interesting!' said Mad Uncle Jack. Before the bearded stranger knew what was happening, Eddie's great-uncle had snatched the watch from his grasp and was studying it closely.

'This watch does indeed belong to my beloved wife Maud,' he mused. 'I gave it to her on the occasion of her twenty-first birthday. Here, read the inscription.'

He thrust the watch under the bearded stranger's chin. When the bearded stranger managed to disentangle the silver watch chain from his beard, he read the inscription:

> To Maud
> Happy 2nd Birthday
> Jack

The bearded stranger frowned. 'Didn't you just say that you gave this to your wife for her twenty-first birthday?' he asked.

'What of it?' demanded Mad Uncle Jack, digging his hands into the pocket of his coat and clasping a dried fish in each.

'Simply that the engraving refers to her second birthday, not her twenty-first.'

Uncle Jack snorted at the bearded stranger as if he

was an idiot. 'It was cheaper to have "2nd" engraved rather than "21st",' he explained. 'You had to pay by the letter.'

'But the "1" of "21st" is a *number*, not a letter,' the bearded stranger pointed out.

'Then I was overcharged!' muttered Mad Uncle Jack. 'Thank you for bringing it to my attention, sir. After we have deposited my great-nephew at Awful End, I will visit the shop where I originally bought this watch for my dear Maud – some fifty-five years ago – and demand my refund of a ha'penny!'

'Yes . . . That's all very well, but that still doesn't explain the reason why I became the target of a watch-thrower!' the bearded stranger protested.

Mad Uncle Jack stuck his head in through the open window of the carriage – his beak-like nose narrowly avoiding poking Eddie's eye out.

'Maud, dearest?' he inquired.

'Yes, peach blossom?' she replied.

'Did you throw your watch at this gentleman?'

'Gentleman? Gentleman?' she fumed. 'He's nothing more than a beard on legs!'

'Did you?'

'I wasn't aiming at him,' said Maud. 'He simply got in the way.'

'That's solved then,' said Mad Uncle Jack, satisfied that the truth had been reached. 'My wife was not throwing things at you, sir. She was simply throwing things, and your head was in the way.' With that, Mad Uncle Jack went to climb back up into the driver's seat on top of the carriage.

The bearded stranger put his arm on Uncle Jack's shoulder. 'Not so fast,' he said. 'This is a public highway and I have every right to be walking down it unmolested,' he said.

Mad Uncle Jack pulled free of his grasp and clambered up the side of the carriage. 'Your head was in the way, sir,' he said. He liked the phrase, so repeated it: 'Your head was in the way.'

'Then be very careful that this boy's head does not get in the way of one of my bullets,' said the bearded stranger.

He opened his coat and pulled out a revolver. He pointed it through the open carriage window, and aimed it straight between Eddie's eyes.

Episode 5

Big Guns

In which we learn that the bearded
stranger isn't either

Now, I don't know if you've ever had a revolver pointed at you, but even if you haven't, you probably know what one looks like.

First and foremost it's a gun. You pull the trigger and, if someone's remembered to put the bullets in it, one whizzes out of the end of the barrel and buries itself as deep as possible in the target.

If the target is just that – a target – then it makes an impressive 'bang' followed by a 'twang' and everyone hurries forward to see how close the bullet hole is to the bull's-eye.

If the target is a person, there's normally a cry of 'AAARGHHH!!!' as well as the bang, followed by a thud as the person falls to the ground with what looks like spaghetti sauce splattered all over his shirt . . . which isn't very nice, especially if your job is to wash the shirt afterwards. In case you haven't guessed it yet, guns aren't the safest of inventions.

The important thing about a revolver is how the weapon got its name. It has a revolving chamber. This means that once a bullet has been fired, the chamber revolves and the next bullet is lined up with the barrel and ready to go. This is jolly useful if you plan to rob a bank or something and want to fire lots of bullets into the ceiling to make people lie on the floor and be ever so helpful. It's amazing how happy even the most unfriendly bank manager is to open his safe when he has ceiling plaster in his hair.

Fortunately, revolvers are also jolly useful for sheriffs and marshals and people like that. They track down bank robbers and lock them away for a very long time for shooting innocent ceilings who never did anyone any harm in the first place.

Anyway, in Eddie Dickens's day, revolvers were one of the newest of new inventions. Before the revolver came along, most guns were flintlock pistols. They didn't even have proper bullets. You filled the barrel with gunpowder, added small metal pellets called 'shot' and hoped for the best.

One of the problems with a flintlock was that you had to reload it every time you'd fired it. This took about the length of time it took for the person you were firing at to come over to you and hit you over the head with the branch of a tree or what-ever else he – or she – could lay his – or her – hands on. An even bigger problem was that a flintlock wasn't very reliable.

If people aren't very reliable, that isn't always the end of the world. They say that they'll meet you outside the cinema at three o'clock, then turn up at half past and the film's already started. It's annoying, but you'll live to see another day. If flintlocks are unreliable, you might not get to the 'living-to-see-another-day' part.

Sometimes, you might pull the trigger of a flint-lock and, instead of the gunpowder firing the shot out of the barrel at the enemy, it would decide to blow up instead: BANG. Just like that.

If you were lucky, it would mean that friends would only have to buy you one glove for Christmas instead of a pair. If you were unlucky, it would mean that you'd never have to bother to buy a hat again . . . because you wouldn't have a head to put it on.

So that's why people who liked weapons thought revolvers were such a good idea – the person you were pointing the thing at was usually the one who got hurt if the trigger got pulled . . . which is why Eddie Dickens was feeling very, very nervous.

'I think you owe me an apology, sir,' said the bearded stranger. 'A simple "sorry" will be enough. Is it too much to ask for?'

'S-S-S-Sorry,' said Eddie, and he wasn't just being polite. He truly was sorry – sorry that he'd ever laid eyes on Mad Uncle Jack and Mad Aunt Maud and her stuffed stoat, Malcolm; sorry that he'd ever had to leave home and go on this dreadful journey to Awful End. Who on Earth would call their house Awful End anyway? His great-uncle and great-aunt, that's who. And why didn't that surprise Eddie?

'V-V-Very sorry,' Eddie added.

'It's not you who should be apologising, boy,' said the bearded stranger. 'It is this gentleman, here, who has insulted me.'

Eddie was tempted to ask the man why, if he – Eddie – had done nothing wrong, he was the one having the revolver pointed at him . . . but he thought it best to keep his mouth shut.

'Put that thing away, you big bush,' snarled Mad Aunt Maud, clambering out of the coach with surprising speed.

She snatched the stranger's beard and, to everyone's complete and utter amazement, it came away in her hand. Only Malcolm the stoat's expression remained unchanged, which, if you think about it, is hardly surprising.

The bearded stranger, who wasn't really bearded at all, made a grab to keep his disguise over his face. As he did so, the revolver was no longer pointing at Eddie, but skywards.

Mad Aunt Maud, who obviously wasn't so mad when it came to dealing with would-be highwaymen, grabbed the stuffed stoat by the tail and swung its head against the man's legs.

There was a nasty scrunching noise as the stuffed animal's nose came into contact with the man's knees, followed by a loud wail which Eddie was to remember right up until his sixteenth

44

birthday. (How he came to forget the wail on that particular birthday has to do with a lady hypnotist called the Great Gretcha, and is another story.) The non-bearded bearded stranger pitched forward, dropping both his revolver and false facial hair to the ground.

As the gun hit the solid roadway, the trigger was knocked back and a small flag on a pole shot out of the end of barrel and stayed there. The flag unfurled and on it was one word.

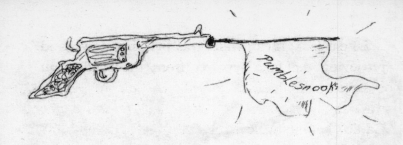

If you thought that the word was BANG then you'd be wrong. That word was PUMBLESNOOKS so you can guess how little the letters had to be for all of them to fit on a flag small enough to fit in the barrel of a gun. But they were big enough for Eddie to read them from where he was standing.

The man with the pretend beard had been threatening them with a *pretend* revolver! Now that the beard was gone and he was rolling around in the mud clutching his knees, Eddie recognised the insulted stranger instantly. He was no stranger at all. He was none other than Mr Pumblesnook, the actor-manager of the band of strolling theatricals.

It soon became apparent to Eddie that his great-uncle and aunt also recognised Mr Pumblesnook, but instead of being outraged, their behaviour amazed Eddie for the zillionth time since he'd left home with them.

'Oh, Mr Pumblesnook, you really are the most remarkable of men,' cackled Mad Aunt Maud, hoisting the mud-covered man to his feet with such force that he almost slammed into the side of the coach.

Uncle Jack, meanwhile, was bending down and retrieving the fake revolver from the road. 'You most certainly had me fooled, sir,' he confessed. 'I was already wondering how we should divide Eddie's belongings between us if you had shot him.' He handed the actor-manager his false beard, which now had a few twigs and a piece of an owl's eggshell in it. 'Where are you headed, Mr Pumblesnook? Might we offer you a lift?'

Eddie was furious. He was fuming with rage. Was he the only one who was outraged at some practical joker having pointed a gun at him? It didn't matter that the gun had turned out to be nothing more than a stage prop, the fear Eddie had felt had been real enough.

'What's this all about?' he demanded. 'Why is Mr Pumblesnook going about in disguise frightening . . . frightening poor, innocent children like me?'

'A *disguise*, my boy?' said Mr Pumblesnook, one eyebrow raised in a most dramatic manner (as far as eyebrows can be dramatic, that is). '*Criminals* wear disguises, my child. *Spies* wear disguises. This is not a disguise, Master Edmund. This is a *costume*. This is me in character.'

'But you're not on the stage now,' Eddie protested, quickly adding a 'sir'.

Now, actors love to quote the lines of a playwright called Shakespeare, not just when they're in the middle of a Shakespeare play on stage, but whenever they get the chance. One of Shakespeare's lines that actors most like to quote is: 'All the world's a stage.' You may not think that it's the most brilliant line in the world – and that you could have come up with it – but Shakespeare came up with it first, and that's the main thing.

Who remembers the name of the second human being to set foot on the moon? Who remembers who came second in last Wednesday's geography test? Who remembers there was even a test? No, Shakespeare was the first one to write these words down and, because they're about acting, these are words actors particularly like to quote.

Think back to Eddie's words just then, and you can imagine how delighted Mr Pumblesnook must have been that he'd just heard them.

For those of you too lazy to look back a page, let me remind you that Eddie said: 'But you're not on the stage now . . . sir.'

No wonder Mr Pumblesnook's eyes lit up. Eddie's comment gave him the perfect opportunity to reply: 'But, in the words of the immortal bard, "All the world's a stage," my dear boy!'

And Eddie was impressed. He had no idea who or what 'the immortal bard' was – he had no way of knowing that it was strolling-theatrical-speak for Shakespeare – but he was impressed by a pertinent quote when he heard one.

'It is important for a great actor to get in character,' Mr Pumblesnook explained. 'It is important to develop a role long before it reaches an audience. Why, when I was preparing for the part of the salmon in *We Little Fishes*, I spent a whole month in the bath and ate nothing but lugworm and ants' eggs.'

He climbed up into the coach and sat next to Mad Aunt Maud, who was back in her original seat. Malcolm was back on her lap, none the worse for wear. 'I remember that time you were preparing to play the part of the kidnapper in *Bound Hand and Foot*,' she said, the admiration sounding in her voice. 'The way you managed to trick the genuine French ambassador down into your cellar and kept him hostage there was a stroke of genius! Such a shame you were arrested before the show could be performed.'

'Theatre's loss,' the actor-manager agreed, shaking his head sadly.

Eddie sat down and closed the door to the coach. He had a terrible sinking feeling. Mr Pumblesnook was obviously a close friend of his great-aunt and uncle . . . and that strongly suggested he was as mad as they were.

Episode 6
Orphanage

In which geese save Rome

Every story is told from a certain point of view. The storyteller – who is me, me, ME in this instance – tells a story in a certain way and sticks to it.

Apart from the occasional trip to Mr and Mrs Dickenses' bathroom, this story has been told from the point of view of staying with poor young Eddie. Wherever *he* goes, *we* go. When he got into the carriage, we went with him. When he spent the night in the stable of The Coaching Inn, we spent the night there too. When he was staring down the barrel of a fake revolver, we didn't run off and leave him there . . .

. . . but let's not be too proud of ourselves for standing our ground. If the revolver had been the genuine article and a bullet had been fired, Eddie would have been the one who was shot and bleeding, not us. I might be able to invent a book that fires a bullet at its readers when they turn to page 46, but imagine the mess it might cause in bookshops or public libraries.

No, the important thing is that nowhere in the story have I said 'meanwhile' and switched the action away from Eddie to somewhere else.

It's perfectly okay to do that in a book. There's nothing wrong with it. There are some really good stories where the author says 'meanwhile' and switches the action to somewhere else . . . but what a good storyteller doesn't do is suddenly change the point of view.

After all this time of not saying 'meanwhile' and switching the action to somewhere else, he doesn't suddenly say 'meanwhile' and switch the action to somewhere else . . .

Meanwhile, back at Eddie's home, his parents were in a state of panic. The reason why the Dickenses were panicking was the small matter of their house being on fire.

Nothing can spoil a late afternoon as much as having flames leaping out of all the upstairs windows, licking at the woodwork. This was a direct result of the latest stage in Dr Muffin's Treatment for their terrible ailment – even hotter hot-water bottles.

The Dickenses were only allowed to get up three times a day. They had to suck special ice cubes and they had to snuggle up in bed with piles of hot-water bottles. When this failed to achieve the desired results, the good doctor decided that their hot-water bottles couldn't have been hot enough.

He solved this by devising a new system especially for them. This system would heat the hot-water bottles while they were actually in the bed with the patients, and Mr and Mrs Dickens were the very first people he tried it out on. As it turned out, they were to be the *only* people he tried the system out on, because he guessed (correctly) that setting fire to those in his care wasn't particularly good for building a bond between any doctor and his patients.

(I say 'his patients' rather than 'his or her patients' because there weren't any women doctors in those days. They weren't allowed. It was something to do with the belief by the Medical Experts With Huge Beards Association that women's hair

52

would somehow get in the way of their stethoscopes when trying to listen to heartbeats. It was a pretty feeble excuse, but the governing body of the Medical Experts With Huge Beards Association really did have very impressive beards, so no one dared argue with them.)

Anyway, back to Dr Muffin and his hot-water bottle heating system. At his home, the doctor had a special tray on the sideboard of his dining room designed to keep food hot. Under the tray were three liquid paraffin burners with adjustable wicks to make the flames bigger or smaller. He took these burners to the Dickenses' house and put them under a bed.

The idea was that the flames would gently heat the mattress, which in turn would gently heat the hot-water bottles, which would, in turn, gently heat Eddie's parents. That was the idea. Of course, when the doctor did his first 'test run' on the bed in Eddie's room (because he was on his way to Awful End and wouldn't be needing it), Eddie's mattress burst into flames.

Fortunately for the doctor, he was holding a hot-water bottle, from which he whipped the stopper and poured the contents onto the mattress and extinguished the conflagration (which is a twenty-eight-letter way of saying what 'put the flames out' says in fifteen).

Eddie's parents could smell the burning but couldn't investigate because they'd already been up three times that day – once to have a sword fight with the Thackerys over at The Grange, once to go shark fishing with the Trollope family who were renting a houseboat on a nearby lake, and once to throw an old boot at a cat that was yowling on top of the compost heap – so they knew they must stay in bed. Dr Muffin would be very angry with them if they got up a fourth time, and might refuse to allow them to pay him lots of money to treat them any more.

'Ish evwyfung awlwhy?' called out Mrs Dickens, who on this occasion didn't have a famous-general-shaped ice cube or an onion in her mouth, or both for that matter. The reason why 'Is everything all right?' came out sounding so strange on this occasion was that she had Mr Dickens's ear in her mouth.

Those of you with a squeamish nature, who feel sick if you tear a fingernail or see an ant walking with a slight limp, will be pleased to know that the ear was still attached to the side of Mr Dickens's head (which was exactly where it should be).

It was simply that Mrs Dickens had been sleeping moments before the goose in their bedroom smelled the smoke coming from their son's room and woke them up with its loud honking. Geese were very popular in the days before battery-powered smoke alarms.

If you think that sounds crazy, go and find a teacher – or some other kind of know-all – and ask them the following two questions:

1. Are a flock of geese really supposed to have raised the alarm and warned the ancient Romans of an attack on the Capitoline Hill by the Gauls in 387BC?

2. Did miners really used to take canaries down the mines to warn them of any gas in the mine shafts?

The answer to both those questions should be a resounding 'YES!!!', so the Dickens family goose smoke alarm wasn't such a crazy idea after all, now was it? In fact, the very first battery-powered smoke detector alarm was a bird, though it was a chicken not a goose. Surely you've heard of battery hens?

So, where was I? Oh, yes: the smoke from Eddie's burning mattress made the goose honk, which then woke up Mrs Dickens. She had been dreaming that she was eating a dried prune, which she discovered, upon waking, was in fact her husband's ear. She called out to ask Dr Muffin if everything was all right and – lying – he assured them it was.

The doctor then refined the method. He realised

that what stopped the flames of the three paraffin burners from burning his food on the sideboard at home was that they heated the metal tray which, in turn, heated the serving dishes which, in turn, heated the food.

So what he did was turf Eddie's parents out of bed and make them sit on one of the thirty-one different types of chair designed to make you sit up straight even if your wrists were handcuffed to your ankles. (There had been thirty-*two* when Eddie left the house, but one had been completely eaten by a hungry woodworm since then. It must have been very hungry indeed, because Eddie had only been gone one night.)

While the Dickenses shared a chair, Dr Muffin rolled back their mattress and placed a number of trays and serving dishes he'd found down in the kitchen on the bed springs. He then rolled the mattress back into place with a satisfying crunch of china. He placed the three paraffin burners on the floor under the bed, made the wicks as big as possible, lit them, then ordered his two yellow-and-crinkly-edged patients back into bed.

'That should keep you good and warm,' he announced. 'You must both stay there until morning,' he said. 'Under no circumstances must you get up unless it is to go to the bathroom. Good day to you.'

With that, he left the bedroom, walked past Eddie's room, where the blackened mattress still smouldered, and made his way downstairs and out of the house. Not ten minutes later, the Dickenses' mattress was on fire.

'Perhaps it's supposed to be,' said Mrs Dickens, a trifle concerned.

'Surely not,' said Mr Dickens, the left leg of whose pyjamas had just caught alight.

'What should we do?' asked Mrs Dickens, the pom-pom on the end of her nightcap glowing like a golden Christmas tree bauble.

'Do? Why, nothing,' said Mr Dickens. 'The doctor has forbidden us to get up under any circumstances.' He had been brought up to respect the orders of a medical man.

'Under no circumstances, unless it is to go to the bathroom,' Mrs Dickens reminded her husband.

'Then let's go to the bathroom!' cried Mr Dickens.

'Good idea!' said Mrs Dickens and they both leapt out of bed seconds before all the paper bedclothes went up in a very pretty WHOOOSH of orange flame.

By the time they reached the bathroom – because they thought it would be cheating if they didn't really go there – it was on fire too. So were the stairs, their bedroom, Eddie's bedroom, the roof and just about everything else upstairs.

'Oh dear,' said Mrs Dickens. 'What shall we do?'

They decided to panic, which made perfect sense under the circumstances, because there wasn't a lot else they could do. The goose, meanwhile, had flown out of the window and was honking to her heart's content.

Talking of "meanwhile" – as I was earlier, if you recall – Eddie meanwhile was sitting on the edge of a metal-framed bed in a dank cell of a huge prison-like building called St Horrid's Home for Grateful Orphans.

Words his wise old mother had spoken came back to him. They were something she'd uttered before he'd set off with Mad Uncle Jack: 'Do be careful to make sure that you're not mistaken for a runaway orphan and taken to the orphanage where you will then suffer cruelty, hardship and misery,' she'd said.

And now here Eddie was . . .

What's really annoying is that we don't know how he got here. We were so busy with our meanwhile-back-at-home-with-his-parents that we missed the main action. Perhaps we'll never find out how he ended up in this godforsaken place. Perhaps we'll find out in the next episode.

In the meantime, we must leave Eddie frightened and alone in his cell, while his parents are trapped upstairs in a burning building.

Sometimes life can be really tough.

Episode 7

Escape!

*In which we finally get back
to poor old Eddie*

'Oh dear, Mr Dickens!' cried Mrs Dickens. 'Whatever shall we do now?'

'Do, Mrs Dickens?' said her husband. 'Why, we shall burn to death, of course.'

'Do you think that was Dr Muffin's intention?' asked Mrs Dickens, beating out the row of little orange flames that were licking at the bottom of her nightgown.

'Well, being burnt to a crisp would most certainly cure us of our dreadful illness,' Eddie's father pointed out.

Anyone eavesdropping on this conversation would never have guessed that these were the same two people who, moments before, had been in a terrible state of panic.

Anyone eavesdropping on this conversation would also have been very hot. The reason why Eddie's parents were suddenly so calm was that they were in the bathroom, and the bathroom contained a cabinet which contained a bottle which contained Dr Muffin's Patent Anti-Panic Pills. Mr and Mrs Dickens had both eaten a fistful.

The reason why anyone eavesdropping would also have been very hot was that the bathroom was now a wall of flame.

The Dickenses' alarm goose, meanwhile, had flown to the nearest house – The Grange, owned by the Thackery family – and was busy telling their alarm goose what had happened.

Here follows a rough translation of the conversation between the two birds:

Thackery goose: You smell of smoke, Myrtle.
Dickens goose: Hardly surprising, Agnes.
                    The Dickens residence has
                    gone up in flames.
Thackery goose: Oh dear.
Dickens goose: Yes. Such a shame.

Unfortunately, all the Thackerys' daughter – who

61

was sitting near the geese at the time – heard was:

Thackery goose:	Honk honk honk honk, Honk.
Dickens goose:	Honk honk, Honk. Honk honk honk honk honk honk honk honk.
Thackery goose:	Honk honk.
Dickens goose:	Honk. Honk honk honk.

Even if she had understood every word the two geese had spoken, this still wouldn't have been much use to the poor old Dickenses trapped in their burning home. Charlotte Thackery was less than a year old and, although she made a wide selection of exciting noises from 'goo' to 'ga' with a 'guck' thrown in for good measure, her doting parents couldn't understand a single word she said.

Fortunately for Eddie's parents, however, help was at hand. Those of you who can remember all the way back to page 4 will recall that the cupboard under the stairs of the Dickens household was occupied by Gibbering Jane.

Gibbering Jane was a chambermaid who had failed the eight-week bed-making course and lived a life of shame in the darkness. She never came out of her understairs hideaway. Food was slipped under the crack between the floor and the bottom of the door and, if you really want to know how she washed and went to the loo, I'll have to draw you a very detailed and complicated diagram which will cost you a great deal of money.

The only other person in the house – apart from Eddie's parents, of course – was Dawkins, Mr Dickens's gentleman's gentleman, who lived in a basket (with plenty of tissue paper) in the kitchen. He's also been mentioned before, but I can't remember the page he first put in an appearance. I do remember that the Dickenses often didn't remember Dawkins's name and sometimes called him 'Daphne', though.

One of Dawkins's duties was to feed Gibbering Jane. He was just passing through the hallway, making his way towards the cupboard under the stairs, when he noticed that the whole of the upstairs of the house was on fire.

Without a moment's thought for his own personal safety, Dawkins knew exactly what he must do. He dashed back into the kitchen and rescued his tissue paper from his basket.

He snatched the paper up in his arms and ran outside with it, leaving it beside a tree (weighed down with half a brick). Satisfied that this was a job well done, he decided that he'd better go back inside and see if Gibbering Jane or his master and mistress needed any help.

'Help!' cried Mr Dickens from upstairs.

'Help!' cried Mrs Dickens from upstairs.

'Are you talking to me?' Dawkins shouted.

'Oo aw yaw tawkin' taw, Dawkins?' asked Mrs Dickens, who had just stuffed another fistful of Dr Muffin's Patent Anti-Panic Pills into her mouth.

Dawkins was well used to his mistress talking with her mouth full and instantly translated this latest communication to mean: 'Who are you talking to, Dawkins?'

'Why, to both you and the master!' he shouted, then coughed as a cloud of smoke billowed down the stairwell.

'Well, we were indeed calling for help from anyone who might hear us and that most certainly includes you, Daphne,' cried Mr Dickens. 'Unless you can help us sooner rather than later, my wife and I are sure to end up dead before the end of Episode 7.'

'Before the end of what, sir?' shouted the gentleman's gentleman, who had no idea that he was a character in a story.

'Never mind, Dawkins,' yelped Eddie Dickens's mother (who, as you can tell from her voice, had now swallowed her pills). 'Just rescue us, will you.'

Dawkins thought this was an excellent idea, if only he could think how to rescue them. He heard some gibbering at ankle height and looked down to see Gibbering Jane. It wasn't that she was so small that she only came up to his ankles – that would be ridiculous. It's just that – apart from Eddie – she was about the most sensible person we've run in to in this adventure. She knew that hot air (which includes smoke) rises, so the best thing to do if you don't want to suffocate is to lie on the floor with a wet flannel over your face.

Gibbering Jane was lying on the floor, but she didn't have a flannel, so she was using a knitted ladder.

In all the years Jane had been in the cupboard under the Dickenses' stairs, she'd spent at least eleven hours and thirty-six minutes a day knitting. To begin with she'd made all the usual things – scarves, tea cosies, bobble hats – but, over time, she'd become more adventurous, knitting everything from fireplaces to ladders.

Dawkins saw the knitted ladder and, without so much as a 'May I borrow this for a moment?' he snatched it from Gibbering Jane's grasp.

This wasn't the sort of ladder Dawkins could climb up to rescue the Dickenses. It was all floppy and would need to be fixed in position upstairs in the first place . . . but if he could somehow get the knitted ladder up to them, Mr and Mrs Dickens could then tie it to something heavy, throw the other end out of the window and clamber down.

'I have a plan!' Dawkins shouted.

'This is no time to be frying eggs!' cried Mrs Dickens.

'He said "*plan*" not "pan",' said Mr Dickens.

'What plan?' shouted Mrs Dickens, whose eyebrows had just been singed off by a passing fireball.

Unfortunately, Dawkins had misheard his mistress's response to mishearing him. He thought she'd said: 'This is *now* time to be frying eggs,' so – being a very obedient servant who never questioned the Dickenses' instructions – he'd already rushed to the kitchen to prepare them a mouthwatering eggy snack instead of putting his rescue operation into effect.

Gibbering Jane, in the meantime, was gibbering – which should come as no surprise – and also crawling across the hall floor to safety. Parts of the upstairs of the house were now joining the downstairs by the quickest route, which was by falling from a great height in burning chunks.

Unless either Mr or Mrs Dickens could come up with a good plan and put it into operation within the next eight paragraphs, there was no way they'd come out of this alive . . . and that way Eddie would *rightfully* be in the St Horrid's Home for Grateful Orphans rather than because of some dreadful mistake.

It was then that Mrs Dickens had a brainwave. She

usually had one every sixteen years or so, so wasn't due to have one for another three. Luckily for them, though, she had this one early. 'The winch!' she cried.

'The what?'

'Follow me!' Eddie's mum shouted, and dashed back onto the landing, the fire raging all around her. Mr Dickens followed her into the bedroom. There, in the corner, was a coil of sheets. These were the same sheets as had been tied together and used to lower their bed out of the window, when they were waving farewell to dear Eddie and Mad Uncle Jack and Aunt Maud.

The reason why the sheets hadn't burnt to a crisp like almost everything around them was that they were soaking wet. It had been raining hard when Eddie's parents had seen his carriage disappearing into the distance. By the time Dawkins had winched the master and mistress back into the room and given them fresh brown paper sheets, the soaking wet coil of knotted sheets which had been used to hoist them up and down lay forgotten in the corner.

The heat of the fire had almost dried the sheets by now, and there was the hiss of the water turning into steam above them . . . but they were still just too wet to burn.

Mrs Dickens grabbed the sheets and tied one end to the nearest heavy thing that wasn't on fire.

Unfortunately for Mr Dickens, that was him and he had to struggle to free himself. He retied the sheets to the metal frame which was all that remained of their bed. The frame was very hot, and

he burnt his fingers, but there was no time to lose.

Meanwhile, Mrs Dickens had thrown the other end of the knotted sheets out of the window.

'Go!' said her husband, urgently, and she clambered down the outside of the house . . . to safety.

Now it was Eddie's father's turn. He had always been afraid of heights, and even felt a bit dizzy when he stood on tiptoe. Once, when he had stood on a chair to reach a book on a high shelf, he had had to be talked down by a team of passing philosophers, brought in by the fire brigade. One of the few things Mr Dickens was more afraid of than heights, though, was fire – so he was out of that window and climbing down the outside of his house quicker than you could say 'how now brown cow', which I've always thought was a rather strange thing for anybody to want to say anyway.

The result was that both Mr and Mrs Dickens escaped from the fire that had been caused as a direct result of Dr Muffin's Treatment. Unfortunately for Dawkins (sometimes known as Daphne), he wasn't so lucky. After trying to reach his master and mistress with the eggy snack that he'd made as a result of a genuine misunderstanding, he was forced back by the flames and had to retire to the garden. There he discovered that a burning ember must have floated through the air and landed on his tissue paper, setting it alight and reducing it to a very small pile of ashes. He burst into tears at this unhappy sight.

Gibbering Jane was equally unlucky. The results of all her years of knitting for eleven hours and thirty-six minutes each and every day were destroyed – except for the top left-hand corner of an egg cosy, which she was to wear on a string around her neck for the rest of her life.

'We're alive!' said Mrs Dickens.

'Thanks to your plan, my dearest,' said Mr Dickens.

'But no thanks to Dr Muffin!' said Mrs Dickens, beginning to have doubts about the doctor for the very first time since the Treatment had started.

Eddie's father was about to agree with Eddie's mother when he noticed that there was something different about her. At first he thought it must be the black soot that was smeared all over her face, but after he had rubbed it off her with the damp sheet that flapped at the bottom of the 'rope', he realised what it was.

'You're not yellow any more!' he gasped.

Mrs Dickens grabbed the sides of Mr Dickens's head and felt them. 'And you're not crinkly round the edges any more!' she said in amazement.

They then sniffed the air. It smelled of burning house and furniture.

'And we don't smell of old hot-water bottles!' they cried, in unison.

'We're cured!' said Mr Dickens and, taking his wife by the hand, they both danced around in a little circle.

'Dr Muffin is such a genius!' Mrs Dickens pronounced. 'I'm so sorry I doubted him.'

At that moment there was a terrible groan and their home came crashing down into a pile of brick and wood that looked nothing more than a giant bonfire.

'This calls for a celebration!' said Mrs Dickens. 'Just think, now that we're cured, there's no need for Simon to stay at Awful End.'

'You mean Jonathan,' said her husband, when, in fact, they both meant Eddie. You will recall that neither of them was terribly good at remembering their son's name.

'We'll send word to your Mad Uncle Jack to bring him back home!' smiled Mrs Dickens.

Little did she and Mr Dickens know that their dear beloved son had never even reached Awful End but was languishing in St Horrid's Home for Grateful Orphans.

Now, you don't really know what 'languishing' means and I don't really know what 'languishing' means, but it's what people do in prison cells or orphanages in books . . . and this is a book, and poor old Eddie is in an orphanage, so 'languish' he must. That, I'm afraid, is the way of the world.

There was a book in Eddie's cell – sorry, room – in the orphanage. Written on the front in big gold letters were three words 'THE', 'GOOD' and 'BOOK', which, if you put them together, says: 'BOOK GOOD THE'. If you put them together in the correct order, they say 'THE GOOD BOOK', which is what I should have done in the first place.

As it was, this was the book that was going to help Eddie escape, but not until a later episode . . . and not until we find out how he ended up in St Horrid's in the first place.

Get On With It!

*In which a chocolate could be
a mouse dropping*

Things started to go from bad to worse for Eddie after the actor-manager, Mr Pumblesnook, joined him and Mad Aunt Maud in their carriage – not forgetting Malcolm the stuffed stoat.

Who could forget Malcolm? Not Eddie, that's for sure, because the stoat's snout was stuck in his ear.

'Why are we all squashed together like this?' he demanded, still angry with Mr Pumblesnook for having pretended to be a villain and pointed the revolver at him. 'Couldn't one of us sit on the other seat?'

This seemed a fair enough question, because all three of them (plus stoat) were sitting next to each other along one seat, while the seat opposite was v-a-c-a-n-t, which spells 'empty'.

'I am in charge of seating arrangements and I say this is how we shall sit!' roared Mad Aunt Maud.

'Did you not, in fact, spend a summer at the Young Ladies' School for Seating?' asked Mr Pumblesnook, who in Eddie's opinion was simply trying to keep in her good books.

'You are correct as always, Mr Pumblesnook,' Mad Aunt Maud simpered, and blushed like a young school girl which – with her age and wrinkles – gave her the appearance of an under-ripe prune. 'I did not, in fact, spend a summer at the Young Ladies' School for Seating . . . My knowledge of seating arrangements is instinctive. I was born with the skill!'

'But this is ridiculous!' said Eddie, who now had the misfortune of his great-aunt's elbow in his ribs, as well as the stoat in the ear.

'Quiet, boy!' screamed Mad Aunt Maud. 'When I was a girl, children were seen but not heard!'

'When I was in my early youth . . .' began the actor-manager, who, you will recall, used many words when few would do. '. . . When I was in my early youth, children were neither seen nor heard.'

'Just smelled?' suggested Mad Aunt Maud.

It was obvious to Eddie that Mr Pumblesnook hadn't been about to say 'just smelled', but he was too polite to say so.

'They were neither seen nor heard, just smelled!' Mad Aunt Maud screamed. 'Rubbed down with an onion so they just smelled!'

The mention of an onion reminded Eddie of his own dear mother, who had recently taken to popping whole, peeled onions in her mouth to improve the shape of her head. You guessed it. This was another part of Dr Muffin's Treatment. He sighed.

'Don't be sad, child,' said the actor-manager. 'Let us take advantage of the many miles and hours we share to see whether you have within you the potential to be a thespian!'

Eddie looked at him blankly.

'We've got time on our hands, so let's see if you can act,' Mad Aunt Maud translated. This was the first sensible thing she had done in the brief time he had known her. Eddie was stunned. So was Mad Aunt Maud. She seemed as surprised at saying something sensible as Eddie was.

'Me, act?' said Eddie, a tingling of excitement starting in his feet. Or perhaps it had more to do with wearing itchy socks.

'Indeed, boy, that is precisely what I indicated. Let us endeavour to establish whether you have the gift!' said Mr Pumblesnook. 'As you saw from my performance when hit by this dear lady's watch' – he nodded in the direction of Mad Aunt Maud, his forehead hitting her on the chin because all three were sitting so close together – 'it is vital to remain in character whatever the distraction.'

'Stay in character?' asked Eddie.

'To be the person whose character you are portraying,' explained Mr Pumblesnook.

Eddie still wasn't sure what he meant until Maud explained: 'Once you're pretending to be a character, don't let anyone put you off.'

For the second time in as many minutes, Eddie was stunned. If Mad Aunt Maud kept on being this helpful, they'd have to rename her Only-Mad-Some-of-the-Time Aunt Maud. What had got into her?

'Acting is so much more than pretending to be a character,' stressed the actor-manager, 'but, in essence, once you become that character you must not, as this fair queen just intimated, let anyone "put you off".'

Eddie did his best not to laugh at the idea of anyone calling his great-aunt 'fair queen'.

At that moment, there was a cry of 'Woooah, there!' from Mad Uncle Jack, and the carriage came to a halt. There was a scrambling sound as he clambered from the driving seat, and then his beakiest of beaky noses appeared through the open carriage window.

'A call of nature,' he said.

'I didn't hear anything,' said Mad Aunt Maud. 'What was it? An owl?'

'No, my dear, what I mean is –'

'Did either of you hear an owl?' asked Mad Aunt Maud turning to Eddie first, an action which led to her hitting him in the face with Malcolm's nose, then, turning to Mr Pumblesnook, hitting him with the stuffed stoat's tail.

'No,' said Eddie, nursing a nosebleed.

'Neither a terwit nor a terwoo, madam,' said Mr Pumblesnook, looking for the piece of tooth that had been chipped off into his lap.

'A badger call, then?' asked Mad Aunt Maud. Both Mr Pumblesnook and Eddie tensed just in case she turned to them again, bringing her stoat with her. Who knew what new injuries she might cause?

'No, my dear! By call of nature, I mean that I have to go to the . . . I must . . .' Mad Uncle Jack's face reddened, though it was so thin you wouldn't have thought that there'd have been room for it.

'Not an owl? Not a badger? Surely you don't mean that boring little bird that has a call that's supposed to sound like "a little bit of bread and no cheese"? Surely you didn't stop the carriage for such a commonplace call as that?' his wife protested.

Mad Uncle Jack was about to do some more explaining, when he could wait no longer and dashed off into the undergrowth. He appeared a few minutes later with a look of relief on his face.

'Did he find the eagle?' asked Mad Aunt Maud, as her husband climbed back up the side of the coach.

'Eagle?' asked Eddie.

'Children should be neither seen nor heard, just smelled!' she cried in indignation, as though she had just thought of it.

Eddie relaxed a little. There was something strangely reassuring about his great-aunt going back to being completely bananas.

'Eagle aside, young fellow-me-lad,' said Mr Pumblesnook, 'let us commence our experiment.'

There was a flick of the reins, a clomp of hooves and the carriage was in motion once more. It was agreed that Eddie was a fine little gentleman. Don't forget that Eddie's parents had spent good money on turning him into a little gentleman. (They'd tried to spend *bad* money on him, but it'd been sent back.) And, being such a fine little gentleman, might it not be a good idea to start his acting by playing the part of a child so different from himself.

'You don't mean a Foreigner?' said Eddie, shocked, when Mr Pumblesnook suggested this. This was in the days when all Foreigners were treated with a great deal of distrust, whether they were a prince or a pauper or anything else that did or didn't begin with the letter 'p'.

'Indeed not, sir!' said the actor-manager, clearly shocked. 'I would hardly ask you – an untrained actor and merely a child, also – to assume the role of a Foreigner in the presence of a lady in such a confined space!'

'I met a Foreigner once,' said Mad Aunt Maud, a faraway look in her eye. 'I couldn't see him nor hear him, but I could smell him . . . someone had rubbed him down with –'

'An onion?' Eddie suggested.

'Good boy,' nodded Mad Aunt Maud. She tickled him under the chin and slipped a chocolate drop into his mouth. At least, Eddie hoped it was a chocolate drop. It certainly looked like one, but, knowing his great-aunt as he had come to, it could have been a mouse dropping.

Chewing the 'thing' somewhat nervously, Eddie leant forward to get a clearer view of the actor-manager past Mad Aunt Maud. 'If not a Foreigner,' he said, 'what part would you like me to play?'

'That of an orphan boy,' said Mr Pumblesnook.

Those of you with long enough memories, or at least half a brain cell, will see that this really marks the beginning of Eddie's latest troubles.

Episode 9

A Serious Misunderstanding

In which we meet the Empress of All China . . .
Well, sort of

'What is the most important thing to remember when playing a character?' boomed Mr Pumblesnook, carefully wrapping a piece of one of his teeth in a handkerchief as he spoke.

The piece had broken off when Mad Aunt Maud had hit him in the face with the swing of her stoat's tail, half a mile or so back.

Eddie, meanwhile, was using his handkerchief for a very different reason – to try to stem the flow of blood pouring from his nose where his great-aunt had hit him with Malcolm's other end (during the selfsame swing). Eddie was beginning to suspect that Mad Aunt Maud could inflict more damage with that single stuffed animal than the average army could with wheelbarrows full of weapons.

'The most important thing to remember when playing a character?' said Eddie, thinking hard. 'To stay in that character, no matter what?'

'Ridiculous!' cackled Mad Aunt Maud, then slouched backwards in the seat of the carriage. She began rummaging in her handbag.

'Excellent!' said Mister Pumblesnook. 'Exactly, my boy. Exactly. There was one time when I was playing the character of a large hazelnut for a production of *Nuts All Around*. The costume was made from genuine hazelnuts, by my own good lady wife.'

'Lazy wife?' asked Aunt Maud, perking up. 'You should poke her with a stick or thrash her to within an inch of her life.' An inch is about two and a half centimetres, but this happened in the old days and, anyway, to thrash someone 'to within two and a half centimetres of their life' doesn't sound so good.

'My *lady* wife,' Mr Pumblesnook explained. 'Now, where was I? Oh, yes. I was playing the character of a large hazelnut when a family of squirrels – which must have been nesting in the roof of the barn we were using as a theatre that night – fell from the hayloft onto our makeshift stage . . .'

Eddie wished that the actor-manager would get to the point, but he knew that there was no

81

point in trying to rush a man who used seven hundred and twenty-three words when eleven would do. (And don't go back and count them. That was just a figure of speech . . . and if you don't know what a figure of speech is, I wouldn't worry too much. I didn't know what a four-wheel drive vehicle was until I was knocked down by one when I was twenty-three years old, and it never did me any harm. Well, it *did*, in fact, harm me when it ran me over, but you know what I mean.)

'Thinking that I was a giant hazelnut, the squirrels proceeded to attack me, and nibbled at my outer shell,' Mr Pumblesnook continued. 'In such a situation a mere mortal would have slid out of the costume and fled the arena, but not I. I am an actor! I am a thespian! I was playing the character of a hazelnut in front of an audience, so a hazelnut I had to remain. It would take more than a marauding gang of tree rats –'

'Pirates?' interrupted Aunt Maud. 'You were attacked by pirates?'

'Not pir-rates, madam,' said Mr Pumblesnook with extreme patience. 'Tree rats . . . squirrels.'

Still dabbing his nose with his bloodstained hanky, Eddie was trying to work out why his great-aunt had suddenly started mishearing things. Why had she suddenly gone a bit deaf? She hadn't had much problem with her hearing for the first leg of their journey, so why now?

'So, the play continued,' Mr Pumblesnook went on. 'I remained in costume and in character, and behaved as a hazelnut would have behaved when under attack from squirrels . . . In character . . . The key to success as an actor, my boy!'

Eddie was about to ask how the average nut behaved when being eaten by squirrels – in a silent, crunchy sort of way, he supposed – when he was distracted by Mad Aunt Maud's actions.

Humming a tune so tuneless that it would probably be illegal to call it a tune in some very strict countries, his great-aunt was trimming her stuffed stoat's nostril hairs with a pair of gold-plated nail scissors. Nothing wrong with that, you might say. There are probably some teachers you can think of who could do with shaving their nose hairs or ear hairs (like Miss Boris, when I was at school) . . . but it was what Mad Aunt Maud was doing with the trimmed hairs that had caught Eddie's attention. She was storing them in her own ears.

All thoughts about nuts had gone out of the window (like his aunt's watch in an earlier episode). No, that's not strictly true. All thoughts of Mr Pumblesnook dressed as a hazelnut had gone out of the window. Eddie was left thinking about another kind of nut: the nut who was sitting there with stuffed-stoat-nostril-hair trimmings in her ears . . . and he was going to have to live with this woman at Awful End until his parents were cured!

He shuddered.

'Are you ready to rise to the challenge, Master Dickens?' asked Mr Pumblesnook. 'Are you prepared to take on the character of an orphan boy and remain in the character – in that acting role – for the rest of this journey? In fact, are you prepared to take on this character and remain in the character until I tell you otherwise?'

'I guess,' said Eddie. It might help take his mind off what lay ahead: life in a strange house with a very strange great-aunt and great-uncle indeed.

'Do you promise to remain in character?' demanded Mr Pumblesnook, leaning across Mad Aunt Maud, who was busy returning the nail scissors to her bag, so – momentarily – letting Malcolm rest on her lap. The actor-manager seized the opportunity of this stuffed-stoat-free moment to look Eddie full in the face, without the fear of a furry sideswipe of tail, nose or paw. 'Do you promise on your family's honour to stay in character ?'

'Yes,' said Eddie Dickens, meeting Mr Pumblesnook's gaze.

'Family honour' was much more of a big deal way back then. In those days, if you punched a bishop or tickled someone collecting money for charity, it wasn't just you who were disgraced, but your whole family.

People would say: 'That's Mrs Harris whose boy ate that statue made out of lamb chops at the art gallery,' and they wouldn't sit next to her at church. Or people would cross the street to avoid walking on the same pavement as any members of the Munroe family, just because Mary Munroe had painted the entire Thompson family bright red while they were sleeping next door. No, family honour was important, so to swear on your family's honour was important too.

And Eddie Dickens had just sworn on the honour of the Dickens family that he would act the character of an orphan and keep acting the character of an orphan until Mr Pumblesnook told him to stop.

Now, Einstein wasn't born when the events in this story occurred, and he's dead now that you're reading this, but it's still worth saying that you don't have to be Einstein to work out what happened. If you've got a good memory, you'll recall that you were first told that Eddie was going to end up in St Horrid's Orphanage for Whatever It's Called as long ago as page 50-something, and this is page 86 . . . so it isn't exactly news. Now, though, we actually come to the moment when events headed in that direction.

Mad Uncle Jack pulled on the horse's reins and ordered: 'Whoa, boy.'

The horse, not used to his master giving sensible instructions, was so surprised that he actually stopped, which was exactly what Mad Uncle Jack had wanted. He had wanted to stop because there was a man with a very tall hat standing in the middle of the road. If Mad Uncle Jack hadn't ordered 'Whoa, boy' and the horse hadn't been surprised enough to stop, the man would probably have been wearing a very squat, crumpled hat by now, and would probably have been somewhat squat and crumpled himself. Mad Uncle Jack had wanted to avoid this because, even in the failing light of early evening, he could tell that this man was a peeler.

Now, you may be forgiven for thinking that a peeler is something you use to take the skin off potatoes, and you'd be right . . . but *this* peeler was a different *kind* of peeler. This peeler was named after a man called Sir Robert Peel and, if you think that this is beginning to sound like a history lesson, then you'd be right again – so I'll keep it short. As well as being famous for being a British prime minister, Robert Peel also founded the first proper police force in Britain, and the policemen were nicknamed 'peelers' after him. If his name had been Sir Robert Bonk, they'd have been nicknamed 'bonkers', so they should think themselves lucky.

So now you can see why Eddie's great-uncle was reluctant to run this man over with his horse and carriage. It was as true then as it is today: policemen get annoyed if you run them over. Especially if you crumple their tall hats.

This peeler's hat – like all peelers' hats – was very tall and thin. It was about as tall as three top hats, one on top of the other. This isn't a very helpful description if you've never seen a top hat. It's a bit like saying to someone that, when your mother sings in the bath, she makes a noise like a Greater Racket-tailed Drongo, when the person you're talking to has never even heard of a Greater Thingummy-Whatsitted Drongo, let alone heard the noise it makes. So, if you've no idea what a top hat looks like, tough luck. This peeler's hat was still the height of three top hats one on top of the other, whether you've seen a top hat or not.

'Good evening, sir,' said the peeler to Mad Uncle Jack. 'Would you be kind enough to step down from your seat?'

He didn't ask to see Mad Uncle Jack's licence and vehicle registration documents, because these hadn't been invented yet – and he didn't ask him to take a breathalyser test, because he wasn't interested in finding out whether Mad Uncle Jack, or his horse, was drunk. This peeler had more important things to do. 'I'm looking for an escaped orphan,' he explained. 'He ran away from St Horrid's Home for Grateful Orphans.'

'Ungrateful swine!' snarled Mad Uncle Jack.

'Exactly what I said,' agreed the peeler. 'I suggested that they change the name to St Horrid's Home for *Un*grateful Orphans, when I heard the news.'

'We must get up a collection to do that at once!' said Mad Uncle Jack, who, once he liked an idea, seized upon it and wanted to act quickly. 'It shouldn't cost too much to change. You simply need to find a local painter to add the letters "U" and "n" in front of the word "grateful" on the sign at the gate . . . I assume there is a sign at the gate?'

'Oh, yes indeed there is, sir,' nodded the peeler.

'Good. I would imagine that a "U" and an "n" would not be too expensive,' mused Eddie's great-uncle. 'I remember having an engraving made on the back of a watch for my beautiful wife some years back, and that only cost a farthing a letter . . . speaking of which, I imagine that St Horrid's has headed notepaper?'

The peeler nodded respectfully. This coach driver was no ordinary coach driver. He was obviously a gentleman.

'So the headed paper will need to be altered from "Grateful" to "Ungrateful", also,' said Mad Uncle Jack. 'No problem there, though. That could be a job for some of the ungrateful orphans themselves. Up at five in the morning, and write a few "Un"s before "grateful"s on the headed notepaper before going up chimneys or down mines or whatever it is the ungrateful little swine have to do for the rest of the day to earn their keep.'

'A splendid solution, sir,' beamed the peeler. After all, it had been his idea to change the name to St Horrid's Home for Ungrateful Orphans, and here was a true gentleman agreeing with him whole-heartedly.

'Let me give you a contribution towards the campaign for such a name change,' said Mad Uncle Jack.

'Well, sir,' said the peeler a little hesitantly. Like all policeman, he had to be very careful about accepting bribes. What one person might see as a genuine contribution towards a legitimate and important cause, an investigating panel might see as a bribe to do – or not to do – something. Then again, the peeler didn't want to upset this fine gentleman by not accepting whatever the amount was he was slipping out of his pocket. Ten shillings? A pound? Five pounds? A dried electric eel.

A dried electric eel?

'I'm sorry I don't have a halibut to give you,' said Mad Uncle Jack, 'but I spent my last one at The Coaching Inn coaching inn.'

The policeman gave him a sideways glance that police officers – men and women – are very good at giving. It's a look which seems to say: 'I don't know what your game is, but I know you're up to something and I intend to find out what it is.' The peeler had never been so insulted in all his life. A dried electric eel? This was the worst bribe he'd ever had. He'd been given half an apple once, but at least he could give that to the police dog back at the station . . . but a dried electric eel? And to think that he'd thought this man was a gentleman!

The peeler's attitude towards Mad Uncle Jack became decidedly chilly. 'I need to search the carriage for the orphan,' he said, dropping the use of the 'sir'. 'Do you have any objections to my doing so?'

'Not at all. Not at all,' beamed Eddie's great-uncle. He had no idea that he had offended the peeler and thought that they were still 'bosom buddies'.

'And who, might I ask, resides within the carriage?' the peeler continued, walking towards one of its doors.

'My wife Maud, the famous actor-manager Mr Pumblesnook and my nephew's son Edmund.'

'I see,' said the peeler. 'And no one else?'

'Just Sally,' said Mad Uncle Jack.

'A maid?' asked the peeler.

'A stuffed stoat,' explained Mad Uncle Jack.

'I see . . .' said the peeler. He looked through the open window in the carriage door to find one side of the carriage completely empty, and three figures and a stuffed stoat squeezed into the other.

He eyed the stuffed animal on Mad Aunt Maud's lap. 'Sally, I presume,' he said.

'Maud,' said Maud.

'I beg your pardon,' said the peeler. 'I was referring to your stoat.'

91

'His name is Malcolm,' said Mad Aunt Maud.

Eddie noticed the peeler raise an eyebrow, and that simple raised eyebrow seemed to say: 'Here's a group of people who haven't got their story straight. They must be up to something. They must have something to hide.' Of course, what the policeman had no way of knowing was that Mad Uncle Jack was mad, and always called Malcolm 'Sally'. Or maybe it was the other way around? Maybe Mad Aunt Maud was mad, and always called Sally 'Malcolm'. Maybe they were both mad, and the stoat's name wasn't Sally or Malcolm but Cornelius or Edna?

'I see,' said the peeler, slowly. 'And who might you be, sir?'

'I,' said Mr Pumblesnook, puffing his chest out

and looking very grand, 'am the Empress of All China.'

You can probably guess what had happened. While we were following the action outside the carriage with Mad Uncle Jack and the peeler, Eddie, Mr Pumblesnook and Mad Aunt Maud weren't sitting in silence until it was their turn again. Life's not like that. They carried on talking . . . and at the same time that Eddie had agreed on his family's honour to stay in the character of an orphan boy, the actor-manager had agreed to take on the character of the Empress of All China . . . and very good he was at it too.

Just because he was facing an officer of the law, Mr Pumblesnook wasn't about to go back on his word and back to who he really was. He had promised to play the Empress of All China, so the Empress of All China he would be.

He didn't have an audience larger than the peeler, Mad Uncle Jack peering over his shoulder, Mad Aunt Maud and her stoat, and Eddie the Orphan Boy, but they were an audience – and this cramped seat was his stage.

'I am the Empress of All China,' Mr Pumblesnook repeated. It's worth noting that, although China was no nearer or further away in miles then than it is today, it was much further way in time.

Today you can jump on a plane to China, or see

the country and its people on television. Back then, few people had been to China or met a Chinese person. Having said that, the peeler was in no doubt that this man was not the Empress of China. This man was a liar.

'I see,' said the peeler. So far he had been confronted by a coach driver who was trying to make a fool of him by giving him a dried electric eel, a stoat called Sally pretending to be a stoat called Malcolm, a woman claiming to be 'Maud', a grown man pretending to be a Chinese woman . . . which left a boy with blood all over his face, dabbing his nose with a hanky.

The peeler pulled a notebook out of his top pocket, and read what he had written only a few hours before on his visit to St Horrid's:

> The Missing Orfan a nasti boy eskaped thur a brokun Winda. There wuz blud on the glass and he musta cut himself.

There was blood on the broken glass . . . and there was blood on the face of this boy, trying to hide himself between two bulky grown-ups.

'And who, may I ask, are you?' the peeler asked Eddie. 'The Czar of Russia? The Queen of Sheba?'

Eddie gulped. 'No, sir,' he said, trying to sound as orphaned as possible. 'I am a poor little orphan boy.'

The peeler leant into the carriage, slid his fingers

94

down the back of Eddie's collar and pulled him out onto the road with one swift yank.

'Gotcha!' said the peeler, with a broad grin. There's nothing a police officer likes more than feeling a villain's collar and, in his book, escaped ungrateful orphans were villains all right. In his book, villains were probably spelled 'viluns' . . . but what did spelling matter at a time like this?

'There's a nice warm cell waiting for you at the police station,' he said. 'Then, after that, you can go back to a nice cold one at St Horrid's.'

'But that's my great-nephew,' said a puzzled Mad Uncle Jack, watching the proceedings with interest.

Eddie managed to twist his head around and look back into the carriage. He looked to Mr Pumblesnook, hoping beyond hope that he would say that it was okay to be out of character now – to admit to the policeman that he wasn't really an orphan – but no such luck.

The Empress of All China gave him a little imperial bow, but said nothing.

'I'm just a poor little orphan boy,' said Eddie, the worry sounding in his voice. His family's honour was at stake here.

'My mistake,' said his great-uncle, losing interest. 'You look just like Edmund and you were riding in my carriage, so I obviously thought you were my great-nephew.' He turned to the peeler. 'Feel free to take him away in shackles,' he said.

'But . . . But . . .' Eddie began to protest. Then the Empress of All China gave a stern cough behind him and he remembered his promise.

The peeler wasn't sure what shackles were. He seemed to recall from Sunday school classes that slaves went around in shackles, so he guessed that they must be those skimpy loincloths slaves were forced to wear instead of proper clothes. He thought he might get funny looks taking the escaped orphan back to the home in a skimpy loincloth, so he clapped him in irons instead.

'Come on, lad,' he said. 'Mr Cruel-Streak will be glad to have you back under lock and key.'

Funnily enough, Mr Cruel-Streak didn't sound like a very nice man to Eddie. And how right he was.

Episode 10

Oh Dear! Oh Dear! Oh Dear!

In which Eddie wants out

Eddie hated the cell in the police station, until he was taken out of the cell, popped into a cosy brown sack and ended up in his room at the orphanage. The room at the orphanage was more like a cell than the cell was. There most certainly wasn't enough room to swing a cat, not that any cats in their right minds would have gone into the room in the first place. They'd have been too afraid of the rat.

Notice that I said 'rat', singular. Not 'rats' as in 'lots'. Just the one . . . and Eddie was sharing his room with it. If it had been a cartoon rat, it would have been wearing an eyepatch and would have had a great big tattoo on its arm. It might even have been chewing a match in the corner of its mouth. Because it was a real rat, it was just enormous and very frightening.

It's true to say that, like wolves, rats have a bad press. Whenever three little pigs' houses are blown down, or a plague spreads across Europe killing millions of people, either wolves or rats get the blame. Rats are, given the chance, probably very nice, clean, friendly, lovable creatures who smell gorgeous and would give half their money to charity if they earned enough. This particular rat, however, was none of the above. This rat was the sort of rat who lived up to the motto of St Horrid's Home for Grateful Orphans.

Now, this would be a good time to tell you what that motto was. It would also be a good time to tell you who St Horrid was. Saints are, on the whole, good people. That's how they came to be saints in the first place.

There was one chap, called Kevin, who became a saint for sticking his hand out of a window. Well, there's more to it than that. He stuck his hand out of the window – probably to wave to a friend or to see if it was raining – and a bird landed on it and, thinking it was her nest, laid her eggs on it. All I can say is that he must have had a very hairy hand, or the bird was very short-sighted.

Anyway, the bird thought his hand was a nest, and sat patiently on her eggs, waiting for them to hatch. The man waited too. Rather than moving his hand he just stood there . . . He stood there until the eggs had hatched and the chicks had grown big enough to fly away. Then, and only then, did our man move.

You can bet your life that the first thing he must have done is rush to the toilet. He must have been there for weeks – with his hand out of the window, I mean, not sitting on the loo. You can be equally sure that he must have had terrible arm-ache. Think how tiring it is when you put your hand up to answer a question, and forget to put it down again (because there's something far more interesting going on just outside the classroom window). Well, he was made a saint.

Another good way of becoming a saint was by having terrible things done to you, but remaining true to your beliefs. Well, someone called St Horrid doesn't sound the kind of person who would be kind to anyone or be very saintly at all really . . . which is terribly unfair.

You see, over time, names change and mistakes get made. There was once a ship called the *Mary Celeste* which was found drifting at sea with no crew on board. It was all very weird and wonderful, and people still talk about it and write books about it to this day – except that nine times out of ten they call it the *Marie Celeste* (with an 'i' and an 'e') instead of a 'y' at the end. Even important reference books, and books written by very brainy people with huge dome-shaped foreheads and thick-lensed glasses call it the *Marie Celeste*, but they're wrong. It's easy enough to find the right name if you go far enough back in the records, but once the mistake was made, it was copied and copied and copied until the untruth became the truth.

The same applied to St Horrid. St Horrid's real name was St Florid, and even that's not strictly true. His real name was Hank, but when he became a saint, he was named St Hank the Florid, and this was shortened to St Florid. Florid isn't short for Florida, because no one had discovered North America yet, except the native North Americans, who were living there quite happily without Disney World or Burger King. No, the word 'florid' means 'having a red complexion' and, in even earlier times, it meant 'flowery'.

In Hank the Florid's case, both meanings applied. Hank was a young lad in the days when kings still had silly names such as 'Ethelred the Smelly' or 'Edward the Nutjob', and he was the son of a woodcutter. (His mother was the woodcutter.

The history books don't tell us what his father did.)
If you were the son of a woodcutter way back then,
you had two choices in life. You either grew up to be
a woodcutter, or you died young.

There were a variety of different reasons for
why you might die. Your lord and master might
kill you for treading on his favourite patch of grass
. . . or you might be sent to fight against some
nasty foreign folk (who were probably really a lot
nicer than your own lord and master, but you'd
no way of knowing) . . . or you might die of some
really unimportant ailment, such as a nasty
cough, because there were no proper doctors or
medicine.

But Hank didn't die young and he didn't
become a woodcutter either. He became a saint.
The lives of saints are always rather hazy because
they were written down a long time after the events
are supposed to have happened, but the story of
how Hank became a saint is well recorded.

One day, Hank was out in the fields watering the goat – not that goats need watering, but the history books are very clear on this point so I thought I should mention it – and thinking about beards. Perhaps he was thinking about beards because goats have beards. Perhaps it was because far more people had beards back then, because no one had invented a decent razor blade yet (or, if they had, they hadn't told anyone else about it). Whatever the reason, Hank was thinking about beards, when he stooped to pluck a single flower from the grass.

He was putting the flower to his nose and giving it a jolly good sniff at exactly the same moment as a queen bee came in to land on it. The queen bee was out scouting for a new home and, if you know anything about queen bees, you'll know that where she goes, all the other bees follow. So, before Hank knew what was happening, a huge swarm of thousands of bees came and landed on his chin and set up home there . . . From a distance, it looked like an enormous beard.

Just then, a huge enemy army came over the hill, and its leader – some books call him 'Simon the Fairly Nasty', and others 'Simon the Not So Nice' – came galloping down towards Hank. The army had only recently landed, and Hank was the first person they had set eyes on from this country. When Simon the Whatever His Name Was saw this man with a huge, buzzing beard that seemed to change shape before his eyes, he turned and fled, taking his army with him.

He's supposed to have said something clever like: 'If the ordinary peasant in the field has such a magical and menacing beard, think how mighty his king must be!' What he probably really said was: 'Yikes! I'm getting out of here!'

Whatever he said, Simon and the enemy army were in such a hurry to leave that they all piled into one ship, instead of the five they'd arrived in, and sank to the bottom of the sea.

Four bees – again, the history books are very clear about this – stung Hank, then the whole swarm moved on (which doesn't usually happen once they've settled), leaving him with a red face and a crumpled flower in his hand . . . which is how he became St Hank the Florid. The saint part came about because he'd saved his country from an enemy in a mysterious fashion, and there were mutterings about 'miracles'. A passing monk had witnessed the whole affair.

Hank spent the rest of his life living in a very comfortable cave called a hermitage, selling pots of honey to passing tourists. All was fine until about 300 years later, when someone wrote down his name as St Hank the Horrid instead of Hank the Florid, and the name stuck. He became known as St Horrid. So people who were nasty and horrid themselves adopted him as their saint, and that must have been how St Horrid's Home for Grateful Orphans got its name.

The motto of the home was 'Work Hard. Get Very Dirty. Be Very Unhappy' and, from what Eddie could see of his room and the rat, it certainly lived up to it. Apart from the rat and his bed – and himself, of course – the only thing in the room was, if you can remember that far back, a large book with 'THE GOOD BOOK' written on the front in faded gold letters.

In Eddie's day, 'The Good Book' was the name that many people gave to the Bible, so that's what he expected it to be. But, when he opened the book, he found that it was full of pictures of . . . Go on. Have a guess. You'll never guess.

It was full of pictures of food. There were big, colourful illustrations of cakes and trifles and fruit salads and pies and every other mouth-wateringly slurpsious things you can think of.

Just looking at it made Eddie feel hungry, and he'd only been in the orphanage a few hours. He wondered how the other poor kids felt – the real orphans – if they had copies of the same book in their rooms. It was like torture, looking at all these good things (lots of them sprinkled with chocolate or with cherries on top), knowing that all you'd get to eat was porridge made from old wallpaper paste, or soup made up from boiling the remains of old leather shoes. (Eddie had been tipped out of his sack and dragged through the kitchens on the way to his room, so he knew what to expect.)

There were teeth marks on some of the pictures and, in a few instances, whole pictures appeared to have been eaten. Eddie imagined the previous occupant being so hungry that he'd been forced to scoff pictures of puddings rather than the real thing. The previous occupant was, of course, the genuinely escaped orphan for whom Eddie had been mistaken.

Because the bag Eddie had been delivered to the orphanage in was so dirty – it must have had coal in it before him – once he was tipped out of it, Eddie would have found it hard to recognise his own reflection. None of the staff seemed to notice he was the wrong boy, and he couldn't rely on his mad great-aunt and great-uncle to get him out of there. What should he do?

Eddie was just beginning to think that there was no hope, when he heard the scrape of a key in the lock and the door swung open. The biggest woman Eddie had ever seen in his life filled the doorway.

He looked up at her.

'Well?' she demanded, anger blazing in her cruel red eyes.

'Not very,' said Eddie. 'You see, there has been some terrible mistake . . .'

The woman hit him over the head with an enormous wooden spoon.

'WELL?' she repeated, but in capital letters this time.

'Ouch! My name is Eddie Dickens. There has been some terrible mistake,' Eddie blurted out, rubbing the lump that was already forming under his hair.

'You know that you are supposed to say "Good morning, good afternoon or good evening, Mrs Cruel-Streak," every time you have the pleasure of my company,' said the woman. She was trying to speak as though she was the Queen of England, but she sounded more like how Eddie imagined the rat would talk, if rats could talk.

'Good morning, good afternoon or good evening, Mrs Cruel-Streak,' said Eddie. 'My name is Eddie Dick –'

Eddie couldn't continue because he found he had an enormous hand around his throat and he was being lifted so high in the air that the bump on his head brushed against the filthy ceiling.

'Where's ya manners, boy?' snarled Mrs Cruel-Streak, dropping all pretence of being queen of anywhere except this terrible place. 'Thought you could run away, did you? Thought you'd get away with it?'

Eddie would have liked to explain that he hadn't run away from anywhere, but all he could say was 'ffrbwllfggghh', which reminded him of his dear mother, who was forever stuffing onions into her mouth, or sucking ice cubes shaped like famous generals. Tears poured down his cheeks.

Obviously delighted that she'd made the boy cry, and satisfied at a job well done, Mrs Cruel-Streak released her grip around Eddie's neck, and he fell back down to earth with a bump.

She then bent down to give the rat a friendly scratch between the ears, in the same way as you or I might pause to stroke a cat. This was a bad move on her part, because Eddie wasn't like the other boys and girls in the St Horrid's Home for Grateful Orphans. He wasn't weak from years of bad food, hard work and no hope. Anyone who could survive a coach journey with Mad Aunt Maud and a stuffed stoat wasn't going to let this bully ruin his life.

Without a moment's hesitation, he snatched up THE GOOD BOOK in both hands, raised it high above him and then brought it crashing down on Mrs Cruel-Streak's head. A look of complete and utter amazement passed across the enormous woman's face, before she slumped unconscious to the floor – and on top of the startled rat.

Eddie decided that it was best not to hang about. He closed the door to his room – let's be honest, it was a cell really, wasn't it? – behind him and turned the key in the lock. The key was on a large iron ring, and hanging from that ring were dozens of other keys. With these keys he should be able to unlock most, if not all, of the rooms in St Horrid's. He could go anywhere. He could free anyone. Yes. That's what he would do. He'd free the other orphans. He'd organise a mass breakout!

Episode 11

The Final Instalment

*In which we rather hope it's
all's well that ends well*

Less than an hour had passed since Eddie had
fled his cell, leaving Mrs Cruel-Streak locked
up inside it, but the change which had come over
the orphanage was incredible.

St Horrid's was usually such a gloomy place
that it would have been more fun to spend an
evening in a coffin with the lid Sellotaped shut, or
to gnaw through your own leg, lightly sprinkled
with salt and pepper . . . but not any more!

There were laughter, whoops of joy and shouting as over a hundred very grubby-looking kids –
who wouldn't have looked out of place in bags of

109

coal, up chimneys or dressed as blackboards at a fancy dress party – were freed from their cells and were now charging all over the place.

Girls and boys who had spent their whole lives 'being grateful', working hard and having a generally rotten time, were now finding out what fun was for the first time. Not that any of them would have recognised the word 'fun' if they'd tripped over it. Reading and writing were actively discouraged at the orphanage. They were thought to be a bad influence.

What use were reading and writing to orphans? All they needed to learn was how to behave, respect their elders and betters, and live on as little food as possible.

In fact, one of the first places the escaped children rushed to was the kitchens, but not to eat. There was nothing you and I would really think of as being proper food in there anyway. No, they poured into the kitchen like a swarm of ants down a crack between paving stones, to give Cook a message.

Cook was a very large man with more warts on him than a toad . . . and the message the orphans gave him was a very simple one. They picked him up as if he weighed little more than a rag doll – there were lots of them, remember – turned him upside down and plunged him head first into a huge vat of bubbling gruel.

You may be sorry to hear that he survived this ordeal and, amazingly, the hot gruel actually cured him of his warts. But Cook didn't know either of these things would happen at the time. All he knew was that the horrible little children who were supposed to be locked in their cells – sorry, rooms – were on the rampage, and that he was now stuck in a cauldron. He was very frightened, and wished that they'd go away. And go away they did.

The army of orphans sensed that victory was in their grasp, but their army needed to arm itself. The obvious weapons were the famous St Horrid's Home for Grateful Orphans cucumbers. These were no ordinary cucumbers. The worst things you can really say about an ordinary cucumber are that it doesn't really taste of much, that it can make your sandwiches go soggy, and that slices can sometimes get stuck to the roof of your mouth.

Not the St Horrid's cucumber. That was a totally different animal . . . which is just a saying, like when some people say that something is a 'totally different kettle of fish'. They don't really mean that the thing is actually a kettle of fish, and I don't mean that the St Horrid's cucumber is actually an animal. When I say that it was a totally different animal, I mean that it was a totally different *vegetable*. Is that clear? Good.

These particular vegetables were grown in the poor, stony soil of the St Horrid's vegetable patch and they were very hard. In fact, they were very difficult to cut. In fact, they were almost rock-solid unless you plunged them into water, brought them to the boil and simmered them for about forty-seven minutes, stirring occasionally.

But the grubby army of escaped orphans wasn't interested in plunging them into water, bringing them to the boil and simmering them for about

112

forty-seven minutes, stirring occasionally. They were glad that these cucumbers were rock-hard, because they made very good clubs – rather like the truncheons carried by police officers, who, you may remember, were called peelers back in the days of Eddie Dickens.

Speaking of Eddie Dickens, what was he up to right there and then? Wielding a cucumber? Stuffing an upturned cook into a cauldron of his own gruel? No, Eddie was working on the next stage of his plan.

It was one thing to get the Grateful Orphans out of their rooms, but he had to try to help them escape from the orphanage altogether. It was all fine and dandy that they should want to get their own back on all the people who had been so horrible to them over the years, but Eddie was thinking beyond that. He had to get them away from this nasty, nasty place and hide them somewhere where they wouldn't be found and brought back.

This is why Eddie was now out in a yard with high brick walls on three sides and a huge locked gate on the fourth. The gate wouldn't be a problem because Eddie felt sure that one of the keys in the bunch in his hand would open it. He was more interested by what was in the yard. It was an enormous float.

I don't mean one of those things that people take into a swimming pool with them when they're learning to swim, or one of those things that bobs around in the top of a milk shake. I mean a carnival float – a large cart that had been decorated to use in a carnival procession. This float had been made to look like a giant cow.

Now, I wouldn't be surprised if the more sensible ones amongst you are wondering what a carnival float designed to look like a giant cow was doing in the locked courtyard of an orphanage. It's certainly the sort of question that would cross my mind if I was reading this story and not writing it. Well, I'll tell you.

The whole idea of the orphanage was to make money for Mr and Mrs Cruel-Streak, but Mr and Mrs Cruel-Streak couldn't really admit that, could they? They had to pretend that the whole idea of the orphanage was to care for the orphans. Now, there was a fairly popular belief at the time that strict rules, hard work and not too many baths were good for orphans, but people would have been horrified to learn that the Cruel-Streaks didn't really care what was good for the children and what wasn't.

St Horrid's Home for Grateful Orphans was paid for by public donations. This meant that people who felt sorry for orphans, or wanted to be seen to care about orphans, paid the Cruel-Streaks to look after them. What actually happened was that Mr and Mrs Cruel-Streak spent nearly all of this money on their own daughter, Angel, or on themselves. The orphans got next to nothing . . . but the public didn't know that.

When you rely on public donations, you have to have fund-raising events, and that's where the carnival float shaped like a giant cow comes in. For hundreds of years, the countryside had been seen as a rather nasty place, full of wolves and highwaymen and people trying to sell you life insurance for your sheep. People much preferred to live in the conurbations (which is a big word for towns and cities).

Recently, however, there had been a movement which said that the country air was good for you and that something equally good to come out of the country was milk. So the Cruel-Streaks had their slaves – the orphans, that is – build them a carnival float that was designed to make people imagine that St Horrid's was a lovely place somewhere in the country, where the lucky little kiddies got plenty of fresh air and milk. Just the sort of orphanage you'd want to give money to, in fact! The float was to be used in money-raising events across the region.

Less than twenty-three-and-a-half minutes after Eddie had first laid eyes on this giant cow on wheels, and discovered that it was hollow, he had rounded up all the orphans and they were piling inside it.

Some of the children were sorry to leave, particularly those whom Eddie had found in Mr Cruel-Streak's office, forcing the poor man to eat blotting paper. They left him tied to his own desk with a cord from his expensive velvet curtains, and with a large paperweight stuffed in his mouth – like a baked apple in a boar's head at a medieval banquet. He wouldn't be able to cry out for help in a hurry.

Now that all of the children were hidden inside the giant hollow cow, Eddie was frantically hitching the float up to a carthorse he'd found in a stable. The horse had obviously been far better loved and treated than the orphans. It certainly had better food. In its stable were a starter, main course and three choices of pudding, along with a selection of fine wines.

Finally Eddie was ready. He had to try several

116

keys in the huge padlock on the gate before he found the right one. It was dark outside by then, but there was still enough of a moon in the sky to see by. Flinging the gate wide, Eddie jumped onto the back of the horse. The giant cow on wheels clattered across the courtyard and out into freedom and the night.

The next morning, when Eddie's great-aunt, Mad Aunt Maud, awoke, she was confused. For some reason or other, she and her husband, Mad Uncle Jack, had spent the night sleeping in their carriage, rather than in some local hostelry, but – no matter how hard she tried – she couldn't remember why.

She had some vague recollection that it had something to do with the Empress of All China, or the actor-manager Mr Pumblesnook and, come to think of it, weren't they one and the same? Hadn't Mr Pumblesnook been pretending to be the Empress, and Eddie pretending to be an orphan?

Eddie? Now, what had happened to that nice young boy? That was it! It had turned out that he wasn't their great-nephew at all, but was really an escaped orphan. He'd been taken away by a peeler, that was it. It was all too confusing.

Mad Aunt Maud's head was in a spin at the best of times, but that morning it was in a whirl. Where was Malcolm? What had happened to Malcolm?

She frantically looked around the inside of the carriage in the early morning light. Her eyes fell on her stuffed stoat and her pulse returned to normal. There he was. Safe and well.

'Good morning, Malcolm!' she said, with obvious relief.

'My name is Jack,' Mad Uncle Jack reminded her, coming out of a light sleep.

'I was talking to my stoat, husband,' Mad Aunt Maud explained, the trimmed stoat hairs having fallen from her ears in the night and restored her hearing. What with her head in a whirl and having slept in an upright position, she had terrible neck-ache. It felt as if someone had stuck a hatpin in the side of her neck.

'But I thought your stoat was called Sally,' he protested. 'I've always called her Sally. Sally Stoat.'

'It is a he and not a she, and his name is Malcolm,' Maud pronounced.

'You never cease to amaze me, O wife of mine,' said Mad Uncle Jack with pride. Pulling a hatpin from the side of her neck, he kissed the spot where it had been.

The pain went almost instantly. 'How did that get in there?' she asked.

'You were snoring in the night and the Empress of All China stabbed you with it,' Mad Uncle Jack explained. 'These Chinese are full of all the

118

mysteries of the Orient. She called it acupuncture.'

'Did it work?' asked Maud with interest.

'After you stopped screaming and we stemmed the flow of blood,' said Uncle Jack. 'I'm surprised you don't remember it.'

'I must admit I'm feeling a little groggy this morning,' said Mad Aunt Maud. 'There's a lot I don't recall. Where is the Empress now?'

Jack looked down to the floor of the carriage and pointed. Mr Pumblesnook was asleep at their feet.

'Another Chinese custom?' asked Aunt Maud.

'More a lack of space,' said her husband. 'Now, if you will excuse me, I must get some air.' With that, he stepped over the sleeping figure of the actor-manager, opened the door and climbed down onto the rutted track . . . and can you guess who or what he came face-to-face with?

No marks for those of you who said 'a giant hollow cow on wheels'. He came face-to-face with Eddie's mother and father, Mr and Mrs Dickens. Their clothes look singed and their faces slightly sooty, but that wasn't what Uncle Jack noticed first and foremost.

'You're not yellow any more!' he said, in obvious wonderment.

'No,' smiled Mr Dickens.

'You're not a bit crinkly round the edges,' said Mad Uncle Jack, stunned.

He stopped and sniffed the crisp morning air with his beak-like nose. 'And you don't smell of old hot-water bottles!' he gasped.

'NO!!' said Mr and Mrs Dickens as one, with big happy grins on their faces. 'Dr Muffin is a genius! He cured us. All it took was burning down our home and everything in it. The combination of chemicals in all that smoke we breathed in was just what we needed. We're fine now.'

'Splendid . . . Splendid,' said Mad Uncle Jack, smoothing down his hair, which was sticking up all over the place after a night spent in the carriage. 'But what brings you here?'

'We're here to collect Eddie,' said Eddie's father. 'We expected you to have reached Awful End by now, but, as luck would have it, we've caught up with you already.'

'Eddie?' frowned Mad Uncle Jack, as though he was trying to remember where he'd misplaced a pair of spectacles or a rather unimportant piece of cheese.

'Our son?' said Mrs Dickens, cautiously, without so much as a famous-general-shaped ice cube or an onion in her mouth to muffle her speech. 'Now that we're cured, there's no need for you to look after him any more.'

'Precisely,' agreed Mr Dickens.

'Ah! I see,' said Mad Uncle Jack. 'The problem is that you were mistaken. The boy you gave over to our care was not your son Edmund at all but an escaped orphan. He admitted it himself. I remember it quite clearly now.'

'Not Jonathan?' said Eddie's mother in amazement. 'I'm sure I'd know if he was my own son or not.'

'How unfortunate,' said Mad Uncle Jack.

At that moment Mr Pumblesnook rolled out of the open door of the carriage, landed with a 'splat' in the mud and woke up with a theatrical roar. 'WHO DARES TO KICK ME FROM MY OWN BED?' he demanded, in capital letters, in the same voice as he'd used to such great effect on the stage when playing Dr Pompous in the popular play *Royal Rumpus*. Then he leapt to his feet.

Eddie's mother and father had never met Mr Pumblesnook before, so were quite intimidated by this big hulk of a man with a barrel chest and booming voice.

'This is the Empress of All China and these are Edmund's parents,' said Uncle Jack, making the introductions. 'It seems that Edmund really was Edmund after all,' he told the theatrical. 'A most unfortunate mishap.'

'My name is Pumblesnook,' Pumblesnook explained. 'I have merely been in the character of the Empress this past day or so. It is indeed an honour to meet the parents of Master Edmund, a boy with obvious –'

'Forgive me for interrupting,' Mrs Dickens interrupted, 'but where is our boy now?'

'In some orphanage somewhere,' said Mad Uncle Jack. 'St Morbid's? St Solid's? St Poorly? I'm afraid I don't recall . . . I wouldn't worry. You can always get a new one.'

'A new one?' said Mr Dickens, puzzled.

'Another boy,' said Mad Uncle Jack.

'Oh,' Eddie's father nodded.

'What brings you to this neck of the woods, sire, madam?' asked Mr Pumblesnook, wiping the mud splatters from his jacket with the kerchief that had so impressed Eddie when he'd first laid eyes on the actor-manager in the stable of The Coaching Inn coaching inn.

'We sent Edmund to stay with my dear husband's

aunt and uncle because we were ill and didn't want him to catch whatever the disease was we had,' began Mrs Dickens.

'But now we are cured, there is no need for him to stay away from us, so we're here to take him home,' said Mr Dickens, taking up the story. 'We caught the train, and planned to walk the last mile or so to Awful End, which is how we came to catch up with the carriage so quickly.'

Mr Pumblesnook wiped away the last of the mud with a dramatic flourish, shook his kerchief and returned it to his breast pocket, where it sprouted from the top like some exotic flower. 'How were you cured?' he asked with interest.

'Our good doctor, the notorious Dr Muffin, burnt our house down with us inside it,' said Eddie's mother, the pride sounding in her voice. 'We don't know whether it was the fear of being burnt to a crisp or the effects of the woodsmoke but, either way, he cured us.'

'A truly remarkable tale!' boomed Mr Pumblesnook, obviously impressed. 'But I do have one question.'

'Yes?' said the Dickenses.

'You say that there's no need for young Master Edmund to stay at Awful End now?'

'Yes,' nodded the Dickenses.

'That he can come home with you after all?'

The Dickenses nodded again.

'But did you not most recently inform me that your house was, in your own words, if my recollection serves me correctly . . . was . . . burnt to the ground?' inquired the wandering theatrical.

Mr Dickens looked at Mrs Dickens. Mrs Dickens looked at Mr Dickens.

'By Jove!' he wailed. 'We hadn't thought of that!'

Eddie's mother let out a plaintive wail and crumpled to the ground. Her husband found that the easiest way to calm her was to fill her mouth with acorns. It reminded her of some of Dr Muffin's earlier attempts at remedy, and it strangely comforted her.

Mad Aunt Maud, meanwhile, was the last to emerge from the carriage. With Malcolm tucked firmly under one arm, the hatpin protruding from the stuffed stoat's nose, she walked around to the front of the vehicle.

Suddenly she recalled why they'd had to spend the night sleeping in the carriage, rather than being driven the last few miles home. They had no horse. It wasn't that Mad Uncle Jack had left the horse in a bathroom, or anything like that, this time. Early on the previous evening the horse had bolted, run away, legged it – call it what you will. Luckily for Mad Uncle Jack on top and the occupants within, the horse hadn't bolted with the carriage still attached. It had somehow broken free and, before Uncle Jack had had time to catch the startled creature, it had run – in the words of a popular little ditty – over the hills and far away.

Note that I described the horse as having been a startled creature. Startled by what? By the Dickenses' faithful servants Gibbering Jane and Dawkins? Admittedly, they did look quite a sight. They'd travelled on the train with Eddie's parents, but, because they were servants, they'd travelled on the outside and were still covered with bits of gorse bush and splinters of telegraph pole that they'd rubbed up against as the train had gone hurtling along. But no, they'd only appeared on the scene the next morning. I'm talking about what startled Mad Uncle Jack's horse the night before.

Mad Aunt Maud knew what it was. She was staring at the culprit right there and then.

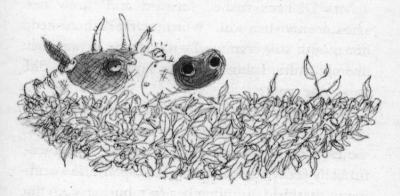

Just over a hedge in a field by the road was the largest cow she had ever seen in her life. The moment she laid eyes on it, she fell in love. It was like the first time she had ever seen Malcolm, in a shop filled with second-hand stuffed animals.

Ignoring all else around her, Mad Aunt Maud stumbled across the muddy road and up to the hedge. On tiptoe she could just reach the carnival float cow's black muzzle. She gave it a friendly pat.

'Hello,' she said. 'I shall call you Marjorie.' She followed the hedge until she reached a gate, then entered the field.

To say that Eddie's parents were surprised when Mad Aunt Maud emerged at the side of the carriage some ten minutes later, followed by Eddie and a crowd of some of the grubbiest children any of them had ever seen, would be an understatement.

Mrs Dickens rushed forward and threw her arms around her son. 'Wurdijucfrm?' she asked, her mouth still crammed with acorns. It was just like old times. I think she was saying: 'Where did you come from?'

Mad Aunt Maud looked far from happy. 'I caught them all climbing out of a cow's bottom,' she explained, a stern look on her face. 'Disgraceful behaviour, if you ask me. Poor Marjorie standing in that field, minding her own business . . . the last thing she needs is a gang of children climbing out of her bottom . . .'

But no one – and I include Eddie – was listening. He was so excited to see that his parents were cured and to hear the news about the destruction of his home. Mr Pumblesnook was delighted by the arrival of the hundred-or-so orphans.

'Young blood!' he said. 'That's what my strolling band of theatricals needs. Young blood! You, children, are my future. Think of all the plays I will be able to perform now with you in the crowd scenes! The audience will love it! Think of the drama of the murder in *Julius Caesar*!'

The children, who had all had a good night's sleep in the giant cow – and hadn't even woken up when Uncle Jack's horse had spotted the monster and made a bid for freedom – were feeling excited and refreshed. They'd no idea what Mr Pumblesnook was on about, because they had no idea that he was an actor-manager, but at the mention of murder they all brandished their St Horrid's Home for Grateful Orphans cucumbers in the air, then brought them down on Mr Pumblesnook in a rain of blows.

'Excellent!' he cried, fending off his attackers with glee. 'You have such spirit!'

And that, gentle readers, is really an end to it and, though this story is called *Awful End*, it was not an awful one for the Dickens family. With their own home gone, Mr and Mrs Dickens and Eddie moved in to Awful End, the idea being that it would be a temporary measure until their own home was rebuilt. As it happened, their family still lives there today.

The escaped orphans did, indeed, join Mr Pumblesnook's band of strolling theatricals and, although they had to put up with Mrs Pumblesnook's irritating way of speaking, and the fact that she still picked the blotches off her face and kept them in the pocket of her dress, it was a good life. Because a big part of being a strolling theatrical is the *strolling* – they were always on the move. The peelers never caught up with them. One or two of the orphans grew up to be very good actors and, if you're ridiculously old, you might even be familiar with some of their names.

Mad Uncle Jack soon tired of sharing his house with Eddie and his parents, so built himself a tree-house in the garden. He made it from the dried fish that he hadn't used to pay his hotel bills. To begin with, he had trouble from the neighbourhood cats, but soon discovered that, once the fish were painted with creosote – which is designed to stop fences from rotting – the smell went and the cats lost interest.

Mad Aunt Maud lived in the garden of Awful

End too or, to be more accurate, she lived inside Marjorie in the garden of her former home. With Malcolm the stuffed stoat, of course. When she died at the ripe old age of 126, she was buried inside Marjorie under the rose bed. There she remained for over eighty-two years, until she was dug up to make room for a swimming pool.

And what of Eddie, the hero of this tale? Well, his adventures weren't quite over yet. History had more in store for Edmund Dickens, saviour of the orphans of St Horrid's. But that, as all the best writers say, is another story.

THE END
for now

The Philip Ardagh Club

COLLECT some fantastic **Philip Ardagh** merchandise.

WHAT YOU HAVE TO DO:
You'll find tokens to collect in all Philip Ardagh's fiction books published after 08/10/02. There are 2 tokens in each hardback and 1 token in each paperback. Cut them out and send them to us complete with the form (below) and you'll get these great gifts:

> **2 tokens** = a sheet of groovy character stickers
> **4 tokens** = an Ardagh pen
> **6 tokens** = an Ardagh rucksack

Please send with your collected tokens and the name & address form to: Philip Ardagh promotion, Faber and Faber Ltd, 3 Queen Square, London, WC1N 3AU.

1. This offer can not be used in conjunction with any other offer and is non transferable. 2. No cash alternative is offered. 3. If under 18 please get permission and help from a parent or guardian to enter. 4. Please allow for at least 28 days delivery. 5. No responsibility can be taken for items lost in the post. 6. This offer will close on 31/12/04. 7. Offer open to readers in the UK and Ireland ONLY.

Name: ....
Address: ....
....
....
Town: ....
Postcode: ....
Age & Date of Birth: ....
Girl or boy: ....

Philip Ardagh Club
token